MRS. S

One for sorrow, two for joy,
Three for a girl, four for a boy,
Five for silver, six for gold,
Seven for a secret never to be told . . .

Also by Jenny Oldfield

Two for Joy
Three for a Girl
Four for a Boy

Animal Alert 1–10
Animal Alert Summer: Heatwave
Animal Alert Christmas: Lost and Found

Home Farm Twins 1–20
Scruffy The Scamp
Stanley The Troublemaker
Smoky The Mystery
Stalky The Mascot
Samantha The Snob

Horses of Half-Moon Ranch 1–6

for S**1**rrow

Jenny Oldfield

Hodder
Children's
Books

a division of Hodder Headline plc

For Kate and Eve. They know why.

First published in Great Britain in 1999
by Hodder Children's Books

ISBN 0 340 74398 0

Typeset by Avon Dataset Ltd, Bidford-on-Avon, Warks

Printed and bound in Great Britain by
Clays Ltd, St Ives plc

Hodder Children's Books
a division of Hodder Headline plc
338 Euston Road
London NW1 3BH

1

You think you want to make it big on TV. It's a way to the fame and the money; you'll be a superstar.

Forget it. Fame can crush you. You imagine you're building an image, but it ends up shaping you and you're trapped inside, screaming to get out. On top of which, everyone starts wanting a slice of your action. They'd kill to get it. Believe me, I know.

My dad, Sean Brennan, works with these people. He produces chat shows for network TV; you know the kind of lurid thing. 'Today's show investigates Men Who Love their Mothers-in-Law (Yuck!), Guys Who Love to Shoot Elk (what do they have to prove?), Women Who Love Too Much (because they're from Venus and Men are from Mars; yeah, right!).

But the little guys and girls who do the confessing aren't the stars of these shows. They make it big on TV for fifteen seconds flat. And there's no money in it, pal.

No, the star is the Host, the Presenter, the Big

Cheese. The huge personality, the giant ego with the fake smile and the lip gloss. The one who can worm the world's worst secrets out of her so-called guests, then turn right around to camera and trash them in front of twelve million people.

I'm talking about Angel here. Angel Christian, owner of Angelworks TV Production Company, multi-millionaire businesswoman, the fifth most famous woman in the United States (they make a league table – they really do). This is her story.

Let's begin with the autopsy. No corpses at this point; that comes later.

The kind of post mortem I mean is staying behind to pick over the bones of Angel's show with a bunch of kids from my class who'd taken up the offer of free tickets, courtesy of my dad. Thanks, Dad.

It was after the event, and Connie, Zoey, me, Ziggy and Carter were hanging out in the studio.

'So,' Connie said, 'if you ask me, they can keep that pile of . . .'

'Yeah, thanks, Con.' My dad killed the lights and turned off the monitors. He'd been working hard all evening. 'Why don't you guys go get a pizza? Kate, honey, I'll see you back at the Square.'

Dad's job depends on everyone being nice to Angel. She can pick up the minutest whiff of negativity floating around the place. It's combustible, like methane gas that blows up in your face. After the explosion, amid the wreckage of egos, you can easily find yourself without a job. That's why you don't call her Valentine's Day show on the hot topic of 'Love Cheats' a pile of . . . well, anything!

'What did I say?' Connie came over all injured innocence.

'I really rated what the big guy with the beard did when he found out his girlfriend had been cheating on him with her office boss!' Ziggy raised his voice as Angel glanced our way. He was like that at school too; saying stuff to please people. Teacher's pet.

The bearded gorilla had jumped out of his chair and punched the girlfriend's boss in the jaw. The whole place went up. Everyone was hollering and standing and cheering. When the camera swung round to Angel, you could see from the little smile on her face that this was good TV. A fight on the set means viewing figures crash the twelve million barrier. Angel counts viewers like a bank clerk counts dollar bills.

'Yeah,' Zoey agreed with Ziggy. She always did. 'The boss deserved a smack in the face, the slimy creep!'

'What about the girlfriend?' I said.

A production assistant was sweeping us out of the gallery, down the metal stairs and across the studio floor like we were garbage.

'A pizza, then home!' my dad reminded me as we hit the exit. 'School tomorrow, remember!'

'Oh yuck!' Connie voiced her opinion of the girlfriend. And school too.

The girlfriend had been Baywatch blonde, with a little girl voice and an IQ that would register even lower than the bearded gorilla's. Sorry about how that sounds. But you know what I mean.

'Like, no way was she worth getting punched in the mouth for.' Ziggy was at it again; agreeing with everything anyone said.

'No girl's worth it,' Carter said, looking at me. That was it from him; short and sweet.

Then, the big moment.

The BIG moment! Angel Christian spoke. To us. To me. She saw us leaving and recognised me from behind.

'Kate, honey!' She broke away from her PA and came across the empty studio. 'How're you doing?'

Angel always speaks to me as if someone just died. When she sees me, she thinks D-I-V-O-R-C-E. Mom

4

and Dad split when I was twelve. That's four years ago, for God's sake. Angel's smile is full of sympathy as she heads towards us; her 'How're you doing?' invites me to crack up and cry all over the studio floor.

'Hey, Angel. I'm good.' I feel about six inches tall because of the way the others are staring at me, especially Carter.

Put me beside Angel and I start eating my heart out.

She's majorly good looking. I mean, the first thing you notice is her eyes. They're huge and dark. Magazines call them almond shaped. They'd say her face was heart shaped. And then there's that thing about bee-stung lips. Yeah; think Angel, think bee-stung lips. Away from magazine-speak, you'd have to admit that the eyes at least hook every single person who ever looks into them. Rich hazelnut brown, with heavy lashes and eyebrows that kind of arch and soar like a bird's wing.

And Angel's clothes. TV clothes. Jade green/apricot pink/dove grey suits with short jackets nipped in at the waist. Velvet collars, contrasting button-trim on the cuffs, plunging necklines, skirts skimming the top of her knees. Businesslike but sexy.

Like the ladies who lunch in downtown Fortune, except Angel never lunches.

She's thin. Very. 'A TV camera adds six pounds in weight to a woman's figure' was her thing. So she never eats. Like I said; does she control her image, or is it the opposite way around?

'How did you like the show?' she asked my friends after the recording of the 'Love Cheats' episode.

'Cool!' Connie and Zoey kidded.

Ziggy came in with an over-enthusiastic 'Great!'

Carter, I noticed, said nothing.

'Good, glad you enjoyed it.' Angel flashed her TV smile. 'And Kate, it's great to see you looking . . . good!'

Lots of empty goods and greats here, you notice.

Like she expected amputated limbs, a scarred face, a bleeding heart. It was only a divorce, for God's sake. I'm fine, Dad's fine, Mom's . . . well, Mom's being Mom in New York, running a private art gallery off Madison Avenue.

'Maybe we should do a show on kids from broken homes.' Angel gazed thoughtfully at me. Well, for her it was thoughtful. Meaning, she paused to look at me for more than a nano-second. 'Would you participate, Kate?'

'Nope.' I didn't plan to be rude. But no way.

'Pity,' Angel said. 'You have a telegenic face.'

Whatever that means.

'Carter would come on,' Connie giggled.

Carter narrowed his blue-grey eyes. 'Yeah, right,' he laughed.

'Carter's parents are still married,' Ziggy pointed out. Ziggy takes things too literally sometimes.

'Whatever.' Angel's smile grew brittle. She glanced round to find her PA absent from her side and panicked. 'Imelda!' she yelled. Very un-TV. More like the kid from Marytown living with her unmarried mother, half-Italian, half-Scandinavian, original name Angelina Christiansen.

That's the other side to this TV megastar. Until she was thirteen years old, Angel lived with her mother in a basement flat in a run-down brownstone house on the wrong side of town. Mom goes to work as a secretary for Jack G Collins, a shoe millionaire in his seventies. Mom marries shoe mogul. Two years later, Jack G dies. Angel and her mom have it made.

'Imelda!' She screams for the PA.

The woman's tied up with some journalist who wants to fix up an interview with Angel, but she cuts loose and comes running. Angel screaming your name is not a pretty sound.

'So, what did you *really* think of the show?' I asked

Carter as the cold air hit us. Zoey, Connie and Ziggy had split off in the other direction to catch the 9.30 Circle to East Village. Carter and I were close enough to walk home through Fortune Park. I live in Constitution Square. Carter's family is in Marytown, which is probably the only thing he has in common with Angel Christian.

'It sucked,' he told me. Not to put too fine a point on it.

We crossed the City Hall plaza, hands in pockets, blowing clouds of steam into the starry night.

'What did you expect?'

'I knew it would suck,' he confirmed. 'It's like we're a bunch of voyeurs getting our kicks from people's private grief. Private except for ten million viewers, that is.'

'*Twelve* million. So . . . ?' Carter doesn't usually take things so seriously.

'Yeah, why go? I know.' He sighed as we began to walk across the park, sidestepping a couple of rollerbladers and a bag lady. 'I guess I thought I might learn something.'

'And did you?'

'Yeah. Everyone cheats.'

Good for a guy to get that lesson learned at the

age of sixteen, then. 'What about the bag lady?' I whispered. She wore twelve layers of clothes all tied up with string, broken boots, a knitted helmet with flaps over her ears.

'Yeah. She cheated on her man,' Carter insisted. 'He threw her out. That's why she's sleeping in the park. Ask her.' He turned as if to backtrack and prove his point.

I panicked. 'Carter, come back!' Change the subject, make him walk along like a good boy. 'How about Angel?'

The bag lady spat on the path after us.

'She cheats.' No doubt about it.

As a matter of fact, she'd just thrown her husband out. Her third: Tommy Jett. She kept the house, Heaven's Gate, and the money; it was written into their pre-nuptial agreement. People were saying wild things about the reasons behind the split, and they all included a third party. No one had any proof though, and Angel sure wasn't talking to the media.

The mystery had added a certain something to tonight's show. Was the megastar who led the discussion about cheating guilty of the crime herself? Or a victim? Watch this space.

'I didn't mean that,' I told Carter. 'I mean, how

about Angel, as in, "do you think she's any good?" '

'The best,' he said. 'Excellent.'

That's the thing about Joey Carter; I never know if he's kidding. I'd expected, 'Nope' or 'She's OK' and a shrug. I got 'Excellent', and the way he said it got under my skin.

'My mom lived in her street when they were kids,' he told me. 'Angel had nothing then, but they all knew it wouldn't always be that way. Show her a gutter and she'd say it was there to climb out of. Tell her she was on the wrong side of the tracks and she'd walk right across.'

'Yeah.' You had to admire that. And it made a difference to how you looked at her now; right at the top of the heap.

'Talking of tracks . . .' We'd reached the park exit. Carter was heading for Twenty-second Street.

I was in the Square, minus the pizza, which we'd overlooked, and by now starving. 'Yeah, see you,' I said.

'You know the guy I thought was real interesting,' he said before he split.

Not the bearded gorilla. Not the office boss who took the punch.

'The thin, nervy one at the back,' Carter told me without waiting for an answer.

It took a while, but then I remembered. The one who never looked at the camera; Brad or Brett something. Black hair, heavy eyebrows, small bony features and eyes that darted here and there. A nervous click in his jawline when his girlfriend spilled the beans: 'I have slept twenty eight times with your younger brother, Johnny.' She'd kept a Cheat's Diary, with twenty eight separate, detailed entries.

The nervy boyfriend didn't hit anyone. He got up and took off, straight out of the City Hall door. No one tried to get in his way.

It was right at the end of the show. No chance to ask the girlfriend for her reaction. The camera had switched to Angel.

'We're right out of time,' she'd told her millions of fans. A guy's world had collapsed. A woman sat looking smug on a lilac leather settee. 'That's it on the Love Cheats from today's Valentine edition of "Angel". Take care, and look out for your friends!'

Angel had signed off with her catchphrase from one more mega-successful show.

Two days later, on February 14th, 'Love Cheats' was networked across America. Two days after that, Angel Christian disappeared.

2

'You gotta be good . . .
You gotta be good . . .
You gotta be good, like you know you should!'

My sister Marcie's voice blasted up from the basement. You wouldn't call it tuneful, but then it wasn't meant to be. Marcie's in a band called Synergie, and tunes don't come into it much. Volume; yeah. Tunes; no.

'You chase your dreams . . .
You chase your dreams . . .
You chase your dreams, that's how it seems!'

Ocean, the lead guitarist in the band, writes the lyrics. My kid brother, Damien, could do it better, and he's just eight years old. But somehow the words, the guitars, Marcie's voice which sounds like she smokes fifty cigarettes a day; they all come out OK. Alanis Morrisette meets Sheryl Crow.

12

I told Ocean he should change his name back to Matt. He'd been thinking River Phoenix, I guess. Marcie says it could've been Leaf or Rainbow, so be grateful for Ocean. I still say change it back.

'Jeez, I gotta get your dad to put soundproofing in that basement.' Mom came into the room where I was watching TV. Something was upsetting her as she flipped stations and turned up the volume on the news channel.

'Hey, that was the Superbowl!' She was interrupting my Thursday night fix.

'Joey, take your feet off the table!' Mom stood in front of me, blocking off the screen. She stood real close to the TV.

I heard the pounding, racing music that comes at the start of the news bulletin, pictured the turning globe, the zooming in on the stars and stripes of America. All I could see was Mom's white ribbed sweater and jeans.

'Here are the news headlines for today, Thursday, February 16th!'

Like, I care. Like I want to know that the Dow Jones is up three points or the bag lady in Fortune Park has won eight million dollars on the lottery. She can buy a new coat and wear it on top of the twelve she already wears. Who cares?

'Angel Christian, America's most famous chat show

13

host, vanished earlier today from her home in Fortune City.'

'Hey!' I took my feet off the table. I stood up so I could see the screen. The news crew was up in a chopper, filming cop cars lined up outside the mansion, and a whole bunch of TV cameras, plus enough journalists to fill a football stadium. The chopper blades rotated with a dry, thudding and grating sound that drowned out the reporter.

'The scene here is pretty chaotic,' the woman yelled. 'What we do know is Angel Christian's disappearance seems to have occurred some time during last night, between the hours of twelve midnight and eleven a.m.' The chopper veered off to the left to give us viewers a fresh angle on the posse of cop cars. The house and grounds looked small, like toy plastic houses on a Monopoly board. 'Eleven was when the alarm was raised. Police say any potential delay between Ms Christian's disappearance and their first involvement in the incident may prove highly significant.'

I was shaking my head. Like, this was some kind of game. How did someone like Angel Christian, the fifth most visible woman in this country, maybe on this planet, just vanish? Click your fingers. Abracadabra.

'Magic!' I muttered. 'How did she do that?'

'Joey!' Mom snapped. 'Just listen!'

Back in the studio, the newsreader was interviewing Kate Brennan's dad.

'Sean, you worked with Angel here at Heaven's Gate all day yesterday. Did she seem to be acting unusually?'

Kate's dad wasn't comfortable on the wrong end of the camera lens. He coughed and shook his head. 'Not really. We worked late, setting things up for next week's show.

'The researchers had been looking for guests who had had experience of violence within the family. Angel wanted to change the angle and focus on female perpetrators of violence. I wasn't sure the women we'd found would give the right message. I was afraid we might be glamorising the whole issue.

'Our discussions went on right up to eleven p.m., at which point Angel's driver came into the studio with what seemed like an urgent message.'

'And that's when she left for home?' The woman newsreader would have made a pretty good prosecution lawyer. She made it look like Sean Brennan had killed Angel Christian himself and buried the body in Fortune Park.

'What's the big deal?' I asked. Take the bag lady; say she was the one who had disappeared. Would she get even two seconds' coverage on national news?

'You keep the score . . .'

Ocean's bass guitar thumped out a dull rhythm from the basement. Marcie's voice sounded sexy even when muffled.

'You keep the score . . .

You keep the score for the guy next door!'

'Sean Brennan, thank you. And now back to Kirstie Schultz at Heaven's Gate . . .'

'I said, what's the big deal?' I could think of a million reasons for Angel to vanish. Think mega-stardom. Drugs, drink, rehab clinics, the taxman. That's four reasons.

'Hush, Joey!' In some way I couldn't figure, Mom was real wound up.

'Kirstie.' The anchorwoman on the news team shot her question and neatly harpooned her next victim: the windblown reporter in the chopper. 'What can you tell us about the present condition of the maid, Rais Sanchez?'

'Rachel, as you know, Ms Sanchez was found in an upper storey bedroom of the house at eleven a.m. After resuscitation attempts were made at the scene of the incident, she was removed to Fortune City General, where she remains in the ICU on the critical list.'

'And we're told there was a lot of blood at the scene?'

A small prompt from Anchorwoman. Alias Ghoulwoman. The voice of America.

'Yes, Rachel. It was a classic stabbing scenario with blood from the victim seeping through the carpet and the floor on to the ceiling of the room below. The housekeeper at Heaven's Gate, Pam Collins, saw the blood and raised the alarm. The rest you already know.'

'Thank you,' Vampire Lady said. 'That's all we have time for. This is the end of the news bulletin.' Now back to the game show/ball game/fifth repeat of Friends, the one where Ross . . .

I looked at Mom, who was crying. 'I was in school with Rais Sanchez . . .' This is what I made out through the tears and snot.

'. . . Fifth grade through seventh grade, I sat next to her in class. We went ice-skating together.'

The maid who was hooked up to tubes and monitors in the Intensive Care Unit. The one whose blood was on the carpet.

Yeah, I could see why Mom cracked up. It would be like Ziggy or Connie lying stabbed in the school corridor. Like finding Kate at death's door.

3

'Hey, Kate, I saw your dad on TV!'

'What happens now Angel Christian took off? Does he lose his job?'

'Does he know what went off at her place? Was he there? C'mon, Kate, you can tell us!'

'Like, I would!' I shook my head and turned my back on them and walked out the school gate. There was two inches of snow on the ground and an icy feeling round my heart after what had turned out to be a bad, bad day.

Like, it's on TV and all the front pages. It's public property. No one thinks what it must be like from the inside.

My dad's down the police department telling them everything he knows. They're scraping every memory cell in his brain to see what they come up with. When I left the house this morning, he was trying to be laid back about everything.

'No sweat,' he said. 'Angel will show up soon, life will go on.'

But I swear his grey hairs have doubled overnight. He has nearly jet black hair, like mine, except at the sides of his forehead. I say he should cut it shorter. When you go grey, the last thing you want is long hair flopping over your face. And it's a nice face. He has straight, dark eyebrows and a way of ducking his head so you can't see his grey eyes. There's always a kind of smile; not so he's laughing exactly. More that he wants you to like him. Anyway, usually he takes my advice. So, I'll push the haircut thing tomorrow, Saturday.

So, I'm looking out for him all day, watching the snow fall, wondering what crummy kind of corridor he's sitting in waiting to see the cops. Thinking, 'It's crazy. What do they think he can give them on top of what he gave yesterday? He explained how he called at Angel's house to see where she was and why the hell wasn't she at the studio – what else is there?'

That was eleven a.m. Which happened to be the time when Pam Collins was hammering on the bedroom door, going crazy about the blood on the ceiling. She thought it was Angel lying on the floor in there. Dad said he had to grab both her wrists then do the slap in the face thing to calm her.

He broke down the door, and they found it was the maid, Rais. Everything was in slow motion until they called the cops and it all went fast forward. Sirens, blue lights, uniforms. Cameras flashing, but no action. Just what looked like a dead body, face down, clothes all slashed, until a forensic guy feels a pulse and says 'This woman is still alive!' and the paramedics show up in the nick of time.

'So where's Ms Christian?' the cops say.

'Search me.' My dad doesn't have a clue.

'Not here!' Pam Collins says. She's checked with the driver, who lives in the gatehouse looking out over the park. The cops go right out to the driver who takes them to the garage, and they find the car missing. Then he cracks up because Rais Sanchez is his girlfriend and they tell him she's the person on the stretcher being loaded into the ambulance.

So now there's one person stabbed and one person missing, and they're all involved: my dad, Pam Collins, and the driver, Stone. They're all at the police department now, giving their statements.

And guys have been going on at me all day long.

'Hey, I saw your dad on TV!'

'He's in the newspapers. Did you see the picture?'

'Did he do mouth to mouth on the maid?'

Connie and Zoey came pretty much everywhere with

me, including recess. Women in Black without the shades. My protection.

Ziggy knew not to say much too. But he couldn't resist, 'Hey, Kate, sorry your dad got mixed up in this.'

I almost yelled at him, ' "Mixed up!" What do you mean by that?' Zoey and Connie steered me into math.

'That's Ziggy,' Connie said.

'Forget it,' Zoey said. 'He don't mean nothing.'

So, it's the end of a truly awful, cold, snowy, freezing February day. My nose is red, my eyes are dry and prickly, like I'm getting the flu.

'Hey,' Carter said, stepping between the gridlocked traffic on West Grand Street.

He'd looped back on himself when he saw me step out of the school gates minus Zoey and Connie. We take the same route home, remember, while the other guys head east of the city. I was seriously hoping that he wouldn't make any stupid remarks.

'Hey.' I sounded real enthusiastic.

'The Blue Bears won 22–20,' he told me. 'Good game.'

I grinned.

My dad rode by at the bottom of State Hill, as I stood talking with Carter. He was telling me about his sister,

Marcie, and her band, doing a pretty good imitation of strumming a bass guitar; *duh-du*, *duh-du*, *du-dum*.

I must have been looking like the Angel thing had never happened.

'Hi, Kate!' Dad leaned out of the car. 'Carter, why don't you and Kate get in and come downtown for a burger?'

Carter looked at me.

'Yeah, come,' I said. 'Why the celebration?' I asked my dad as we climbed in.

'I'm a free man. Free, man. They didn't arrest me.'

'Well, Ah sure am glad 'bout that!' Joke back at him, don't let him see what kind of lousy day I've had. Relief warmed up that icy hand that had been gripping my heart.

'But where the hell is Angel?' Dad rocked his head from side to side to ease the tension in his neck. 'So, Carter – got any theories?' Dad asked.

'About what, sir?'

'C'mon, Carter, don't give me that. About Angel. About absence of Angel to be more precise.' He was packed tight in the gridlock, nose to tail with buses and trucks. Overhead, the Circle train zipped by.

'Could be a kidnap.' Carter mumbled his opinion.

Dad glanced in his overhead mirror. From the back

seat, I could just see his eyes in a shallow oblong of reflective glass. 'Say more.'

'Angel's got mega-bucks,' Carter said. 'Everyone knows Angelworks is worth millions.'

'So, kidnap Angel and you stand to cut yourself a big slice of that pie. And you mean business. You plan the whole thing to get at her during the night when everyone's asleep.'

'What about security systems?' Dad asked, sliding left into the next lane, circumnavigating a yellow bus.

Carter thought hard about this. 'You get inside help.'

'Yeah, go on.'

Carter warmed up. 'OK, so it's going really well. You've got into Angel's room, probably carrying guns. You put a tape over her mouth and tie her up. But the maid hears a noise. You're on the way out, halfway downstairs and she comes out of her room. You lose it —'

'So you lose it and shoot the maid.' It was my turn to cut in. The idea of eating a burger was beginning to turn my stomach. 'That's the natural thing if you have a gun in your hand. So how come Rais was stabbed, not shot?'

'OK, so that needs to be looked at,' Carter agreed,

head to one side, nipping his bottom lip with his even top teeth.

Carter's cropped haircut suited him somehow. Just because I note these personal details, it doesn't mean a thing, OK?

'Somehow the maid ends up making a mess of the bedroom carpet,' he says. He knows he's making my stomach turn. 'The kidnappers get the hell out and no one suspects a thing until nearly noon next day.'

'Hm.' Dad pulled into a McDonalds drive-thru. We joined the line, watching big white flakes settle on the warm hood and melt. 'Two questions.'

'First, how come Angel's car is missing from the garage?' I cut in. BIG point, unexplained by Carter's theory.

Dad nodded in his mirror at me and Carter on the back seat. 'And second, if kidnap's where we're at, how come there's no ransom note?' he said.

I wasn't the only one who didn't enjoy my burger. Dad, Carter and me put them half-eaten back into the polystyrene tray and dumped the whole lot in the garbage.

'Let's see if the cops will let us in to see Angel's sister,' Dad said.

'Sister? What sister?' Carter got on great with my dad. He talked more than usual, asked questions, stopped mumbling.

The traffic had eased as we zapped under the Circle where Fortune Park ends and Marytown, the original Italian quarter north of the city centre, begins. A three lane highway running right around the park took us along two sides of the vast green square to some of the most expensive real estate in America.

'Angel Christian has a sister,' Dad insisted. 'A stepsister, if you want.'

'So what's this my mom tells me about Angel and her mom living in the basement of a brownstone row house?' Carter wouldn't let it go. 'No sister; just Angelina and Momma, and Momma putting her darling in dresses with frills and bows and taking her to dancing auditions at the City Hall or entering her into Little Miss America contests?'

'All true,' Dad admitted. He pulled in alongside the FCPD tape-barriers erected around the entrance to Heaven's Gate. 'But then, if your mom tells it right, Marianna Christiansen went up in the world and took Little Miss Angel along with her.'

'Shoes!' Carter cut in. 'The guy was in shoes.'

'Right.' Dad frowned out at the two cops guarding the entrance to Angel's place. 'Jack G Collins.'

Click. The light went on. Collins. 'Jack G had a daughter, right?' I leaned forward and gripped the back of his seat. 'Pam Collins, the housekeeper here, is really Angel's stepsister!'

No way, like *no way* would anyone have guessed.

Angel was small, thin, delicate as a bird. A multi-coloured, glossy bird always preening and saying, 'Look at me!'

Pam is big. Actually, not much more than five ten, but she feels taller than six feet. Pam is what feels like six feet of solid muscle and bone. And delicate is not what she is.

Angel was (I already talk about her in the past tense) so sure of herself she kind of lit up a room.

I don't think a single person would notice if Pam walked in. Being tall, with reddish-brown hair and green eyes, you would think they would. But Pam had half a lifetime's practice in making herself invisible. She wore sludgy, mud-coloured clothes and no make-up. Her hair could have been wild except she wore it scraped back.

Which is weird because, according to what Dad told

us while we waited for the cops to let us in to visit, Pam was Jack G's flesh and blood, his only daughter and ten years older than Angel. Yet the old millionaire left his house, his shoe empire and all his money to Marianna. Not a cent to the natural daughter. He died and made young Mrs Jack G Collins a happy lady. Floating on her cloud of who knows how many millions of dollars, Mrs Jack G found a corner in all her mansions for mousy Miss Jack G. Wherever Marianna and Angel went, Pam went too. Fine, everyone said. That's great. That's what Jack G would've wanted.

But not for Pam to go along as unpaid housekeeper. Which is what happened. It was like the reverse of the cuckoo story; the bright little bird coming into the clumsy, dull bird's nest.

And soon, because Angel shone so bright in the Fortune City social sky and was a heavenly child, everyone forgot that Pam was the natural daughter. She became The Help.

Which is how she answered the door to Carter, Dad and me.

4

The TV was playing in the office. Pam Collins had the volume on max when me, Kate and Sean walked in. A guy in a yellow golfing sweater was sitting on a blue striped settee discussing the ethics of the confessional chat show with a psychology professor at Harvard.

Ethics? Right or wrong to you and me.

'Is there any single area of a person's private life which you regard as off-limits for the chat show host?' Yellow-sweater asked.

The psychologist gave him some stuff about personal space being emotional as well as physical. 'We all need to protect and respect personal space,' was what she said.

'I just called Fortune City General,' Pam told Sean after she'd hit the button and killed the volume. 'They say no change; Rais is still in ICU, still critical.'

The Woman the World Forgot was dressed in a big grey sweater and black trousers. Her long red hair was pulled back messily, her face was drained, like she'd been at a funeral. What she'd been through in the last twenty four hours was so big it had wiped away all expression.

You were left with a pale canvas, all angles and shadows, a mouth set in a hard line, eyes that didn't blink.

'Did she regain consciousness yet?' Kate's dad walked around the room, flicking through papers on a desk, checking e-mail. Habit of a lifetime spent working for Angel.

'No way,' Pam sighed. 'The cops are there by her bed, waiting.'

Sean tapped the keyboard. 'I guess they want an ID on her attacker from her when she wakes up.'

'It figures. Once they know who stabbed Rais, that will give them the lead they really want.'

One suspect for two crimes; the attempted murder of the maid and the kidnap of Angel Christian. *Presumed* kidnap. Like everyone else, I was jumping ahead.

I looked at Kate. I couldn't read her expression. Was she thinking the same as me? That millions of people out there wanted to hear Angel was safe and well. But how many were praying for the maid to live?

My mom and a couple of others in Marytown. Rais was single. Her parents were dead. There was Angel's driver, Stone, who was also Rais's boyfriend. I guess he wanted her not to die.

Kate was staring at her dad, following his every move. I couldn't blame her; after all, the guy was gonna be high on the list of suspects. Anyone involved in the scene of the crime always is.

'Did the hospital tell you anything about how long before she comes round?' Sean asked. His fingers fumbled with the keys, the screen crashed.

'Like, they would!' Pam managed half a smile. 'Look, Sean, we don't know how long Rais had been lying there. She lost a lot of blood. As far as we knew when we found her, she was dead already. I looked for a pulse, remember!'

'We should've tried to revive her.' Sean's head dropped down. Kate went and stood beside him. 'That was one thing the detective asked me yesterday down at the police department; why didn't we make any effort "to resuscitate the maid"?'

'Don't think that way.' Pam listened to the buzz of the intercom; another visitor had come calling. For a while she ignored it. 'We did what we could. We were in shock. The cops know it.'

I watched Sean get it back together for Kate's sake. 'Sure, you're right. You know, even if Rais regains consciousness, I think there may be brain damage. If they see her as their best lead to Angel, they could be disappointed.'

I watched Pam's reaction to this; like, I wasn't part of the action, I was stepping back and observing. I do this. Watch, listen, try not to get involved.

So, Pam nodded with what looked to me like relief. If I read the expression that flitted into her green eyes right. Like, 'Brain damage? Yeah!' When really, it should've been, 'Brain damage? Oh no, poor Rais!' The two women lived in the same house, didn't they? If you can call Heaven's Gate a house. More like a whole condominium, if you want to know. Corridors, suites of rooms, offices, a fitness centre and a swimming-pool in the basement.

The buzzer gave up and fell silent.

'So, how come the cops aren't following other leads?' Kate asked Sean. 'How come they waste time asking you crazy questions?'

She wasn't standing back like me. She was right in there, worrying like crazy about her dad. Besides, Kate is kind of . . . innocent. No, forget that. She likes stuff to make sense, to have reasons for happening. She works a lot on logic. OK, I guess that's one type of innocence.

'Believe me, honey, they are. They hauled in detectives from all over the state on to this case. It's high profile. The city's crawling with TV cameras. They gotta find some answers.'

Pam's eyes closed to hide what she was thinking. She'd noticed me watching her, see. I thought, this is not the way I'd be acting if my stepsister had disappeared and I'd found the maid in a pool of blood. But Angel was no ordinary stepsister. Nothing here was normal.

Sean went on with his theories, being up front to help Kate, I guess.

'The cops brought their forensic guys in here yesterday and they're still working as we speak. They're networking appeals across every state in America, asking the kidnapper to come forward with terms for Angel's release.'

'That's the optimistic scenario,' Pam said, her back towards me, her voice suggesting that there was more.

So we all stared at her, waiting.

'What if there is no kidnapper as such?' she asked, eyeballing Sean.

Kate took hold of her dad's hand. 'What are you saying?'

'I'm saying this guy, whoever he is, is brutal, maybe even psychopathic. You saw how many times he stabbed Rais,' Pam reminded Sean. 'Picture this; he's some kind of nut who thinks he has a reason to abduct Angel.'

'A stalker?' Kate had been following this closely. 'Like the ones you read about. It happens when you're famous like Angel; a guy trails you, waits outside your house, sends you letters and flowers, then gets upset when you don't answer.'

Sean nodded. 'Pam has a point. The way the guy sees it, you're his sole property. Ignoring him is a big insult. He's gotta punish you. The stalking gets worse, he plans a big hit, lays in wait.'

Think way back; celebrity stalkers. John Lennon. Mark David Chapman kills him and turns right round to say he was the one. That's some five minutes of fame.

'So he abducts Angel because in his crazy eyes he owns her.' The possibility was making Sean shake his head and lean back against the desk. 'He holes up with her and wants her to play house; to be nice, be his.'

'Yeah.' Pam parted the Venetian blind and glanced out of the window. Then she left the room, dropping in this last bit almost casually. 'Angel tells him no way. She lets the creep know that he's crazy. This isn't part of the plan. He still has the knife he stabbed Rais with. Nothing we would call a conscience to hinder him. Love turns to hatred. Adoration becomes blind rage . . .'

She left us standing.

Forget the ransom note. Expect another corpse. No;

rewind. Expect the *first* corpse. Rais is still lying in City General with tubes and monitors keeping her alive.

Imelda Cabasin was the visitor on the buzzer.

Angel's PA had reported in for an evening's work even though there was no boss around to be a personal assistant to. Failing to get anyone to open the door, she'd gone off to find help in the shape of Stone, the driver who lives in the house at the end of the drive, who brought her back to the big house and used his key to get her in.

Imelda acts like the disappearance of Angel Christian is a natural disaster. Like a volcano has erupted and killed three thousand people. Like a hurricane has flattened the whole of Florida. She's choking back the tears, smudging her mascara, hugging people.

'Kate, I'm out of here,' I said. My aim was to slide out and meet Ziggy at 7.30 in East Village the way I'd planned. Pam Collins's Ice Maiden act was one thing. Imelda In Tears, Tragedy Queen, was another. 'How about you?'

'I'll stick around,' she told me with a quiet, sad smile. 'Say hi to Connie and Zoey from me if you see them.'

Stone took me out of the house. He wasn't saying a word and I realised I only knew two things about him. One he drives – drove – for Angel. And two, he's Rais's guy. I didn't even know his other name.

He walked me down corridors, across a yard towards a side gate.

If he'd been hoping that it would steer me clear of the press pack, he was wrong.

Cameras flashed, they pumped questions at me and him.

'What's going on in there?'

'What did the forensic guys turn up?'

'Any ransom demand?'

'How's the maid? Harvey, how's Rais?'

'Harvey'? How come journalists knew Stone's first name? And hadn't these guys ever heard of personal space?

They even followed me down West Grand Street until I came to State Hill.

'I'm nobody,' I told them. 'I don't know nothing.'

East Village isn't like Marytown, though both quarters of the city were built a hundred years back. Where I live on Twenty-second Street is smack in the middle of the old Italian quarter; grocery stores on every corner, bakeries down back alleys, the brownstone rows partly boarded up and graffitied. Kids sit on stoops outside peeling doors, jousting you with their eyes as you walk down the sidewalk. They knock you down with a look unless you get in first with a wisecrack. That's your armour: a joke, a shrug, a walk that says 'Don't mess with me'.

In East Village, on the other hand, the streets have trees. There's the Picasso Coffee Shop on Ginsberg Avenue, live jazz music every night at Armstrong's, huge loft conversions overlooking State Hill and Fortune Park.

The looks you get in East Village are different too. They come from college students outside the bookshops and micro-chip nerds inside the new glass tower blocks; they say, 'Hey you; why don't you crawl right back under that stone you just crept out from?'

On a Friday night Ziggy and me like to upset the college students by walking down Ginsberg Avenue looking like we never read a book in our lives. Picasso who? Wasn't he my sister's first boyfriend, drove a truck for the meat market, ended up running a Mexican place on Twenty-seventh Street?

Ziggy and me met up and cruised the Avenue. Everything was the same: the cafes serving cafe lattes, the jazz bars attracting guys with beards and girls with glasses. But tonight I was different. I was working hard to stop myself from worrying about Kate and Sean Brennan. Or, to be honest, to stop myself thinking about Kate. Not that I was; honest, that is. When Ziggy asked me how Kate was, I chewed him up good: 'Why ask me? How should I know?' That's how not-honest I was.

'Let's go,' Zig said. It was still early, not much past nine thirty, but he'd given up on me for the night.

I shrugged and followed him up to the stop for the Circle train on the corner of Ginsberg. There was one other guy in the shelter, and at first I took him for what he looked like: a bum.

The train came and we let the bum on first.

'Ticket!' the driver barked.

Bum fumbled in his pockets, allowing Zig and me to slip by, as we thought.

'You two; tickets!' Driver spotted us.

We all fumbled for change. Zig and I paid then caught the tickets that the machine spat out. Bum went on swaying and turning out his pockets. A couple of passengers let the driver know they were bothered by the bum.

'C'mon, buddy.' The train guy softened his tone. He wasn't gonna be hassled by no passengers. 'You sit down where I can see you, OK. You find your dollar and you pay me at the next stop.'

Bum didn't so much sit as lurch into a seat opposite Zig and me.

'Hey!' Ziggy knocked me with his elbow.

I pretended to fall over with the pain. *Ouch! Ow!*

'That's . . . that's . . .!' Ziggy hissed, pointing at the bum.

By now the other passengers were getting interested.

'Nah!' Someone shrugged it off. 'No way. You gotta be joking.'

So I began to look hard. What seemed like a bum might not be. He's dressed in an old black leather jacket with a sheepskin collar, all scuffed to hell. His streaked yellow hair is black at the roots; he has three days of stubble on his chin. The eyes are out of focus and bloodshot. He's a mess.

'That's Tommy Jett!' Ziggy came out with it at last.

He got there a split second before me and the rest of the train.

'Hey, Tommy!' A girl called from way down the carriage. 'Where's Angel? What've you done with her?'

The whole train went deadly quiet. *Click-click-clickety-click*; wheels sped along metal rails. The driver shot us a backwards glance.

Tommy Jett heard and lifted his head like it was real heavy and hard to control. Angel Christian's ex glared at me from under drooping lids as if I was the one who'd mentioned his wife's name. From fumbling and swaying like a hopeless drunk, he suddenly shot out of his seat and launched himself at me.

I put up my arms to cover my face. Maybe he had a knife there. It was life-flashes-before-your-eyes time. I saw smashed, drink-crazed eyes, smelt whisky breath, thought of Mom and Pop, Marcie, Damien and me at Disneyworld in a holiday photograph we had in a frame by the TV.

Then I felt Ziggy shove me sideways, so that Tommy Jett crashed down, hit his chin on the empty seat and slid to the floor. He was swearing and rolling in the aisle as the train lurched to a halt at the next stop.

The driver was on the phone, calling an emergency number. I was pulling myself free from Tommy as he tried to grab my legs, kicking his arms and chest.

'Get him off the train!' a woman yelled, fit to burst her lungs.

Easy to say when you were fifteen feet away. Not so easy when the guy had your legs in a tentacle grasp. I remember thinking, 'Don't kick him too hard.' Don't ask me why, but I really didn't want to hurt him bad.

But anyhow, the cop cars were already speeding under the flyover in response to the driver's call. You think it's only in the movies: the squealing tyres, the blue lights, the slamming doors. Tommy Jett heard the cops down below and let me go. He started crawling towards the exit; like if he stayed down on all fours they wouldn't see him.

The sliding-door opened, the cold air hit him in the face and he rolled down the step on to the platform.

'Here he is! Here! Over here!' A dozen people helped the cops make the arrest.

There were feet on the metal stairs, uniforms at the far end of the platform and Tommy was pushing himself upright, reeling against the metal barrier, climbing up and slinging one leg over it.

'Oh my God!' the 'Get him off the train!' woman yelled. 'He's gonna jump! Stop him, someone!'

There was a drop of fifty feet on to the freeway below. Ziggy and me leaped off the train after him. It was *our* turn to grab *his* legs.

He was half over the barrier, swearing and yelling. Four cops were running along the metal platform. Me and Zig hung on to him.

'It's Tommy Jett!' Loud Voice screamed. Tell the whole world, why don't you?

The cops piled in with the cuffs and guns. Within seconds they'd wrenched Tommy back into the land of the living and had everything under control.

No plunge into oblivion, then. Instead, lots of empty time in a cell to sober up and face what he'd done.

Whatever that was.

Ziggy and I gave our statements to the cops along with fifty other passengers who had suddenly played a major part in Tommy's arrest. Then we went home.

Next morning, Saturday, I got up and heard on the News that they'd charged Tommy Jett with attempted homicide.

5

'Great!' I thought when they arrested Tommy Jett. Seriously. I didn't think I was such a horrible person, to feel glad about something like this.

But it put everyone else in the clear, including my dad. Not that I had the slightest, smallest suspicion about him being involved in Angel's disappearance; the cops did though and that was the point. When he came into my room at eight in the morning and told me about Tommy, I could see a cloud lifting and light shining through. No more fumbling in the dark, suspecting the wrong people.

Yesterday, at Heaven's Gate I'd even had my doubts about Pam Collins. I find her quite scary anyhow, in the sense that you can never tell what's going on with her. Like, she strips herself of all reactions. You never get a smile or a frown when she opens the door. But when your sister has been abducted and you've scraped the maid up off the floor, you expect – well, a response.

I could tell Carter saw it that way too. He watches

people a lot, including me. He seems to forget that it works both ways; I watch him watching. Some day, if he's not careful, I'll face up to him and say, 'So?' Like, 'Give me a score out of ten!' Let him know it's unnerving but I can ride it out. Then again, I wouldn't like it if he lost interest completely.

I guess he finds things about me not to like. He thinks I've had life too easy until now. So if Angelworks folds over Angel's disappearance and Dad loses his job, maybe Carter will come over with the sympathy. If . . . if . . . if. Meanwhile, there's this sudden Tommy Jett thing to talk to him about when I see him at school on Monday.

'C'mon, get dressed,' Dad said to me. 'I'm meeting Imelda at Heaven's Gate to work out what to use for next week's slot. I guess we'll transmit a repeat of an earlier show. Move it, move it; we got work to do!'

It was great to be hassled by him. I kidded him that I wanted extra time in bed, so he could hassle me some more. Then the phone went, and it was Mom.

'. . . Hi, Kate honey. How are you?'

'Good,' I mumbled through toast and jam. Dad was feeding me breakfast as I spoke.

'And how's Sean taking the heat after Angel's latest

little stunt?' Mom never disguised her dislike of Dad's mega-star employer.

It was one reason for their split, I guess. She was always bugging him to move on and find a new position. He told her he had one of the best production jobs in TV and planned to stay right where he was.

Mom was jealous of Angel, if you want the bottom line. Dad said that was crazy, and I believed him. There were rows. It grew into an excuse for Mom to leave. I knew that wasn't the real reason; it was like she needed a framework; an exit out of her boring marriage into the world of fine art and galleries. That's her scene. She made it, and I guess she's happy now.

'It's no stunt,' I told her. 'Didn't you hear about Rais?'

'Yeah. It looks like she walked in on something, poor girl.' Mom didn't stop to ask me what I knew. She gave me her version of events, like it was the Bible. 'So how come they waited all this time to arrest Tommy? We all knew he was the one the minute the story broke. It was so obvious. I told all my clients.' (Mom doesn't have customers in her art gallery; she has clients.) 'It's down to Tommy, I said. Remember him at the movie premiere last month? That was just before he and Angel split, but there were rumours already.'

'Mom, I'm real busy,' I broke in.

Dad had tapped his watch and picked up his car keys.

She ignored me. 'There they were at the premiere, putting on an act. No one was fooled for a second. You just had to watch their body language when they stepped out of the limo. No eye contact. Angel froze him out of all the photographs. Then, of course, there was the Incident!'

Mom drew out the word: 'In-ci-dent!' She meant the fight after the movie, when Tommy punched a photographer. He was way out of line, but then that wasn't unusual. Tommy trashes hotel rooms and smacks people in the face on a regular basis. Only this time, he went too far. He spent the night in a police cell and next day Angel announced the split. Or 'The Split', as Mom would say. Upper case letters. Her brown eyes would be wide open, her red lips pursed. The Split.

'It was over long before that,' she told me; the voice of the prophet, although she'd never even met Angel's latest husband. She was off the Fortune City scene before he appeared. But, 'Hear me, oh ye little people!' 'Angel was mixed up with the male lead in the movie, for God's sake, so taking Tommy to the premiere wasn't exactly a tactful move on her part.'

'Gossip and malicious rumour,' I told Mom before I put the phone down. Funny, I felt a twinge of sympathy for Tommy Jett. I didn't know him well, but I'd come across him from time to time, when I visited Heaven's Gate with Dad. He seemed like an OK guy, except when he was smashed.

I went to Heaven's Gate now and kept my head down while Dad and Imelda ran through videos of past shows. I browsed the internet, reading fans' reactions to their favourite chat show host's disappearance on the Angelworks website. 'Devastated,' one said. 'It's like losing a member of our own family.' A guy in Des Moines, Iowa swore he'd seen Angel down his shopping mall the night before. 'Like, yeah!' A cynic from Colorado Springs came on-line. 'Angel Christian is gonna walk into your local branch of McDonalds and ask for a burger!'

'How about we re-run last year's Christmas Special?' Imelda suggested from across the office.

Pam stood by the door, saying nothing about the morning's developments. She'd just brought coffee on a tray and stayed to listen.

'The one we did on body image?' Dad shook his

head. ' "Slave to a Size 8"? Nope, not weighty enough at a time like this.'

Not weighty enough. No pun intended. The joke slid over everyone's heads except me.

'OK, let's go back to last summer.' Imelda pulled another video from its case and stuck it in the VCR. This morning the tears were gone and she was brisk and businesslike, convinced that it wouldn't be long before the cops got Tommy to confess where he was hiding Angel. Then this exercise in setting up a re-run to cover next week's slot would prove a waste of time; Angel would be there in the flesh, interviewing guests about episodes of domestic violence. ('So, Karen, what makes you stay with a guy who beats you to a pulp on a regular basis?')

As Pam came across to the window near to where I sat and slid her long fingers between two slats of the blind to look out on to the front lawn, I risked a remark. 'So how come the cops knew where to find Tommy?'

'He was picked up on a train.' Her answer didn't quite fit the question. She seemed distracted by something happening out there. 'They say he was trying to jump off the Circle train by Ginsberg Avenue. Two kids stopped him falling fifty feet to the ground.'

'What did he tell them about Angel?' This was the big question.

'Big fat zero.' Pam's technique of squinting through a blind was professional; like she'd done it a lot. 'The detective I spoke to last night said Tommy denied it all. His story is that he hasn't seen Angel in over a month. I put the cop straight about that.'

'How come?' I looked up from my screen and caught Pam's face in profile; if anything *more* blank from this angle, with her straight nose, her thin upper lip, the colourless skin.

'I said he was here Wednesday.'

'When, Wednesday?' The day Angel had vanished. This was the first I'd heard.

'Wednesday morning, before Angel set off for the studio. I had to answer the door and let him in because Angel changed all the locks after she threw him out.'

'And what happened?'

Pam shrugged. 'The usual stuff. There was an argument about Tommy's share in the house. Angel said to speak to her lawyer. Tommy trashed a few things. I called Stone to have him ejected.'

'She never mentioned it to Dad.' I'd have known if she had. He would've told me. As far as I knew, Angel had worked all through Wednesday like nothing had

48

happened. 'So why not fill them in earlier?'

'Hmm?' Whatever was happening out on the lawn was taking most of Pam's attention.

'Why not put Tommy in the frame from the beginning?' This seemed close to withholding vital evidence, or whatever they call it.

'They never asked me. Anyhow, I don't think Tommy's the guy they want.'

Since when did the victim's stepsister make judgments for the police? Her answer left me speechless and made me stare out of the window with her while I tried to figure it out. Then I saw what was so interesting.

Stone – Harvey Stone – was in a fight with two journalists. The guys with cameras must have found a back way in, avoiding the security barrier at the front gate. Angel's driver had obviously found them taking pictures of the house or hanging around waiting for some action.

He'd done what any six foot two inch employee of the rich and famous would do to a couple of punks with zoom lenses. He'd put them on the deck. But it looked like they kept on getting up one at a time and coming back at him. There was a lot of swinging fists, grunts and groans, which Pam was watching with interest.

Just as I tuned in, Stone finally socked first one, then the second journalist with punches that put them down for good. Then he turned and stormed towards the house.

'Pam!'

You could hear his bull bellow from way off. Doors banged. Dad and Imelda looked up from their work. Angel's stepsister gave the smallest grimace, almost undetectable.

'Pam!' Stone's voice grew even louder. Then he burst into the office.

'Harvey.' Her voice warned him to get back under control. ('Harvey', not 'Stone'.)

'Those guys are saying she's dead!'

No way could he rein himself back. He was sweating, bleeding from the mouth, crying real tears.

This is where the corpse comes in. I warned you.

'Angel!' Imelda stood up with a strangled cry and tipped her chair over. 'Oh please, God, no!'

My dad rescued the chair before it crashed.

Stone looked wildly round the room. 'Not Angel, stupid! Rais!' He said 'Ray-is' with a southern drawl. 'They just called the hospital and news there is that she died!'

'Oh, man!' Imelda sighed.

We all felt in our bones it was true.

Homicide. Not attempted, but achieved. Murder One. That was what Tommy Jett was facing now.

I sat down hard and stared at my screen. The e-mails about Angel were coming in fast. Read them. Ignore Imelda passing out by the VCR. Cut off from Stone's face disintegrating before my eyes. Do a Pam Collins; cauterize your reaction before it overwhelms you.

'We're praying for you, Angel,' a girl from New Hampshire wrote. 'Tomorrow, Sunday, my church will say special prayers for you to come home safe.'

'One for sorrow,' said the next message. It was unsigned. Some kind of joke or puzzle.

'You know the old rhyme. One for sorrow, two for joy, three for a girl, four for a boy. Apply it to the Angel Christian situation. Get it?'

What was this? Some kind of crazy guy? Who needed magpie riddles at a time like this?

'Play a game with me. A counting game. But count backwards; three-two-one. Today, Saturday, is day three, get it now?'

Before I read any further, I felt my skin begin to creep. 'Dad!' I whispered. 'Come and look at this!'

'So tomorrow, Sunday, will be day two.'

Dad was reading out loud over my shoulder, catching up with me. Pam was trying to shut Stone up. Imelda was out of it in the far corner of the room.

'And Monday will be day one, the e-mail message said. One for Sorrow as far as Angel Christian fans are concerned.

'But think of it a different way; come Monday there'll be one more angel in heaven. Monday, twelve midnight. Nice and clean and neat. The Star ascends. Angel is looking forward to it, I promise!'

6

The news was all over the TV before Kate came up to Marytown to tell me. It broke into the Superbowl coverage and called a temporary halt to Marcie's rehearsal in the basement. Ocean, alias Matt, raced upstairs to watch the newsflash. 'Countdown to Murder' was the way Rachel Jones announced it. It's a great, attention-grabbing line.

'Man!' Ocean said, invisible behind his dreadlocks. ' "One more Angel in Heaven!" That's some weirdo!'

As soon as Mom had heard that Rais was dead, she'd grabbed Damien and told him to bring his skateboard to the park. 'I can't watch this!' she'd said. ' "New development in Angel Mystery!" "Murder Threat against TV Star!" It's like some kind of freak show.'

So my kid brother got hauled off to the park in the snow. Oh yeah; it started to snow midday. They forecast five inches and temperatures three below.

On TV, Kirstie talked to Rachel from outside the missing star's home. The broadcast was live, in the snow.

'Rachel, the question everyone is asking now that the

sinister message came through on the internet is, where does this leave Tommy Jett?'

'Exactly!' Rachel in the studio, protected from the icy wind that blew through Kirstie's light cotton coat, sounded real serious as she recapped the situation. 'The news is out that Tommy did visit Heaven's Gate on the morning of Angel's disappearance, and we know the background: the sudden end to the marriage, the subsequent rows over money, which all provide motives and opportunity for him to be the one. And the police must have been sure of their ground before they made the arrest.'

'Yes, Rachel, but everyone here is saying that the evidence against Tommy is pretty circumstantial. And they wonder how the police department will react in the light of this new development.' Kirstie's voice was high and excited, surrounded by a whole bunch of clamouring reporters sending out similar bulletins to their channels.

I was sliding lower and lower in my seat. It was down to me and Ziggy that Tommy was in that police cell in the first place. Since it happened I'd been praying for anonymity and hoping that they'd let him out. To me it didn't make sense that they'd arrested the guy on not much more than the fact that he was Angel's ex.

Then Marcie answered the door and brought Kate in.

At that point, I wanted to slide under the chair and out of sight. Not because the room was a mess and I wasn't wearing any shoes, but because of the look she gave me.

It said 'Help!' Like we'd both been dragged into something huge and I would know what to do. I didn't.

Kate usually looks cool. Her hair can be down round her shoulders or back in one of those clasps. She can dress casual, which she mostly does, or smart, which I personally don't like so much, but hey, who am I? The point is, today was not one of her cool days.

Marcie looked from me to Kate and back again. 'C'mon, Ocean!' she said with an edge in her voice that made her sound like Mom.

He shook back his locks and shuffled out, down to the basement. 'Weird,' he said.

I stood up. 'Take a seat.'

Kate shook her head.

'Coffee? Pepsi? OJ?' Wow, my manners are excellent.

'No . . . thanks.' She sat down after all, while I cleared newspapers and magazines from the floor and turned down the volume on the TV. 'What's happening, Joey?'

'You tell me.' She was the one with the father working for Angel. I was the one on the outside, being in the wrong place at the wrong time.

'This is out of control. I don't understand.'

'What does your dad say?' Stay focussed. Don't look at her eyes. I did, though, and they were real scared.

'His guess is they'll have to release Tommy after they've interviewed him. They have to wait for him to be sober, from what we hear.'

'Yeah, he was really smashed.' I let slip the fact that I was there. How stupid can I be?

She flashed me a look and I had to tell her everything about the train and Ginsberg Avenue.

'So, you helped them pick up the wrong guy.' For the first time today I saw her smile. 'Nice one, Joey!'

'So why are you here?' If I'm laughed at, I don't react well. My kid brother knows that and does it all the time to bug me.

'I'll go.' Kate stood up. She's as tall as me but ten, fifteen pounds lighter. She has one of those figures that mostly follow straight lines: shoulders, arms, long, long legs. But there are curves too.

'Sorry,' I muttered. The hardest word. 'Look, if Tommy is the wrong guy, that means the cops still don't have a clue where Angel is. And the one hope they had was that Rais would be able to give them a lead.'

She nodded then hung her head. 'Which leaves a million possibilities.'

I switched the subject fast, picking up what was coming through, low volume, on the TV. They were running a thirty minute special on Angel Christian, re-playing her shows and telling her life story, talking about her as if she was dead already. 'How serious is this internet guy?' I asked.

'Who knows? But say he is; deadly serious . . .' Taking a deep breath, she spelt it out. 'This weirdo plans to kill Angel in just over forty eight hours' time!'

So, that helps the focus.

'Carter, there's something else . . . I was there this morning when Stone heard about Rais. There was a whole lot of stuff going on, but I did catch something I guess I wasn't meant to.'

'Which was?'

'Pam telling him to cool it. She said it was true Rais had died in the ICU. She'd never woken up and anyway even if she had they said there was brain damage. Pam told Stone there was no need to worry, to play it cool, say nothing.'

I got a picture of the two of them huddled in a corner. 'And you want to know exactly what they're trying to hide?'

Kate nodded. 'We know Stone was involved with Rais, which leaves him out of the picture. No way would he stab his girlfriend, even if he *did* have a plan to abduct his employer.'

One of the things about Kate I mentioned before is this real methodical side to her. Her face is dead serious. You can almost see her brain working. I let her go on.

'But say the affair turned messy. Rais ditches Stone for another guy, say. He's the jealous type and he can't stand seeing Rais around the place with the new boyfriend.'

I have a new picture in my mind of Stone the Driver, Stone the Bodyguard. There's plenty of him: muscle and fists, shades and a grey uniform when he drives the limo. He could be the jealous type.

'It reaches flashpoint on Wednesday night. Stone fights with Rais in her bedroom, goes crazy and stabs her. Then he panics, thinks he's killed her. He's due to collect Angel from the studio at City Hall, which he has to do before he has chance to move the body.'

Kate mapped it out real nice. I was beginning to believe it.

'My dad says Stone came in in a hurry with an urgent message for Angel. He drove her home and that was the last time anyone saw her.'

'So Stone gets her back to the house before midnight, planning to wait until Angel's in bed then get rid of Rais and clean up.' I was into this now. 'Only it doesn't work out. Angel thinks he's being weird, hears noises, whatever. She walks in on him in Rais's room, sees the blood, starts yelling and screaming. He panics again and that's when he dumps the maid and grabs Angel instead. Like, an accidental kidnapping. It wasn't meant to happen.'

'At the age of twenty, Angelina Christiansen changed her name to Angel Christian and began her meteoric rise.' A well groomed guy on the TV did the biography. There was a still photo of Angel before she was famous, looking somehow unfinished: no make-up, an ordinary hairstyle, a suspicion of the camera.

'Her first job in TV was as a researcher for one of the biggest chat shows in America, hosted by Paul Matthews. Within a year, Angel had ousted her boss and filled his slot in the schedules with her own show. 'Angel' hit our screens and became a phenomenal overnight success, thanks to her blend of glamorous charm and what TV critics have described as the common touch.

'Here was the girl from the wrong side of the tracks who had made good by tackling the issues that affect all our lives: divorce, unfaithfulness, all kinds of little lies and deceits that threaten the way we live.'

Yeah, we know all that. The programme was a waste

of time. It didn't help Kate and me figure out where Angel was now.

'I have a couple of questions,' I told her when she got to the part where Stone had abducted Angel by accident. 'Like, where does Pam Collins figure in all of this?'

'I don't know,' Kate admitted. 'Maybe she slept through it all. Maybe she walked in on it at some point and decided to help.'

'Help kidnap her own sister?' This was a new one. I took some time to think about it.

'Maybe.' Kate jutted out her chin, determined to make these last pieces fit the jigsaw. 'If you were Pam Collins, wouldn't you hate Angel and do anything to get back at her? And remember what I overheard her say to him this morning. And it was Pam and Stone who so-called discovered the so-called body when my dad got there next morning. Boy, must they have panicked when they learned Rais wasn't actually dead!'

'Yeah,' I admitted. Major panic time.

'And!' By this time, Kate was almost yelling. 'Yesterday it was Pam who tried so hard to put Tommy in the frame!'

'Sure.' I couldn't argue with any of this. But . . . just, but! 'Second question: how did Stone react when he heard Rais had died?' I meant, like a man who had just been presented with a Murder One rap, or like a guy who had lost his girlfriend?

Kate paused. 'He cried,' she told me with a wobble in her voice.

Harvey Stone cried. To me that looked like grief. I broke it gently to Kate. Sorry to destroy your latest theory, but I have to say I think Stone is innocent.

So, you can be wrong.

The guy in the smooth suit on TV was up-to-date with Angel's life story by now, telling us how many millions of dollars she was worth.

What good was all the money in the world to her now? OK, it was a cheap shot, but I bet it was what a lot of people watching thought too.

'Paying a ransom would not be a problem to Angel Christian,' Mr TV Smartass told us. 'But therein lies the difficulty. As the hours pass, and no demand for money comes through, there seems to be an increasing lack of logic about the whole situation.'

He made a significant pause. The camera closed in. 'If profit isn't the motive, what is? If the sender of the e-mail is not just some off-the-wall joker and is for real, then the police are faced with a terrific, well nigh insoluble problem!'

'Yeah, forty eight hours to track down a psychopath!' Kate muttered. It looked like she'd given up the Harvey Stone line of investigation after what I'd said.

'So, if you're out there watching this,' the presenter said to camera, 'we're gonna close this special programme with a clip from Angel's last show, the Valentine edition called "Love Cheats".'

Angel's theme tune started to play, soft and low in the background.

'And while you watch it, whoever you are, wherever you are, bear in mind that folks all over America are praying for your victim.' Significant pause number two. The voice lowers to a whisper, like he's talking one to one. 'And, please, find it in your heart to let Angel go!'

Cue volume on the theme music, cut to Angel on her last show shoving the mike under a wannabe Baywatch babe, the type the researchers always dig up. The girl's name is Anita something. She flashes her lashes at the camera and speaks in a little girl voice. 'I slept twenty eight times with your younger brother, Johnny!' she announces, swivelling her big blue eyes.

Angel swings the mike around to get the boyfriend's reaction. I remember this part real well: the boyfriend with the dark hair and heavy eyebrows, the nervy, jumpy, intense one.

'Brett, what d'you want to say to Anita?' Angel chirps. Little bird preening. Little, glossy woman.

'Brett Roberts' – I read the caption under the guy's face. 'Brett doesn't know that his girlfriend slept with his younger brother.'

He did what I would've done. He jumped up and turned his back, walked right out of the studio. He came up the aisle near where Kate, Ziggy, Connie, Zoey and me sat.

'We're right out of time!' Angel told us. 'That's it on Love Cheats from today's Valentine edition of "Angel".'

Cue theme music and credits. One more back view of Brett Roberts making his silent exit. Back to Angel smiling at camera. Her eyes hook you. They're brown and deep. They convince you she's sincere. 'Take care and look out for your friends!'

Fade Angel's face to see-through ghost.

Kate sniffed and turned her head away.

A newsflash broke in before the start of the Australian Tennis Open. Rachel Jones again, putting in extra hours.

'News just in from Fortune City Police Department. The detective in charge of the Angel Christian investigation has just issued this important statement to the press!'

Switch to a grey-haired guy with a moustache sitting

at a table with a blue cloth, a glass of water, a bank of mikes. He clears his throat.

'The results of forensic testing have led to a major leap forward in this case,' he told the watching millions. 'Fingerprint work allowed us to establish earlier this afternoon the identity of at least one person present at the scene of the assault on Rais Sanchez.'

The cop, Sergeant Fiegel, paused to glance round the room. Even he has a sense of timing, for God's sake.

'Bloody prints on the coffee table and on the door handle match up with those of Ms Christian's driver, Harvey Stone. We've had Mr Stone under surveillance for some time and now we have duly placed him under arrest, pending further investigation.'

7

So why did the e-mails keep on coming through?

'One for Sorrow 2. Saturday February 18th, 7.20 p.m.'

'Kate!' Dad called for me to switch off the computer and come and make myself some supper. He'd been on a rollercoaster of emotions all day, like the rest of us; I could hear it in his voice.

'OK!' I yelled back. I was about to come off line anyway.

'One for Sorrow 2.' The second message was unmistakable. 'The countdown continues. Three, two, one. Time flies when you're having a good time.'

'Dad!' I felt sick in my stomach. 'He's doing it again!'

'Such a good time, watching the cops vanish up their own – well, y'know! Forgive my crudeness. First Tommy Jett. Now Harvey Stone. "Harvey who?" you may ask. Stone's the driver. Forget him, he's a nonentity.

'The great thing is, it keeps them happy. I tell Angel all the latest news. We laugh about it together. Well, Angel would laugh if she got the joke. I'm a little disappointed. I find she has no sense of humour.'

'Dad!' God, this was sick. The world was reading this stuff.

He came running and groaned as he read it. 'You gotta hope this is a joke!' he breathed.

'So, let me tell you how Angel and me — no, that should be how Angel and I, I guess — got it together. Wednesday night, I left a message with Stone. Like I said, Stone's the runner; a nobody. It was a message he couldn't fail to deliver and it brought Angel into my waiting arms.

'I dumped Stone at Heaven's Gate and whisked Angel away in a white limousine, tres romantic! No Chevy to the levy; way too downmarket for Angel Christian. This was a Mercedes to Hades.

'And where's that? Well, that's for you adoring fans to work out before Monday night if you want to save Ms Superstar. "Oh honey, that's what you are." I'm talking with Angel there.

'You should've seen the look on my Angel's face when she realised I'd come for her. Somewhere beyond delight, beyond ecstasy — you might almost say it was horror in those beautiful brown eyes. Just for a moment, before she saw how great we'd be together. That was two whole days back. Now she likes it. She loves it, believe me.

'She counts every minute, every second we spend together, knowing it can't last.

'This is the sad part. Every romance must end; even mine and Angel's. Shakespeare knew that. "Parting is such sweet sorrow, that I shall say good night till it be morrow!"

'Good night, good night, my sweet Angel. And as she and I both like to say, "Take care and look out for your friends!" '

Dad dragged me away from the PC and called Zoey and Connie to come over and share my pasta.

'Girltalk!' he said when they arrived half an hour later, kicking the snow off their shoes and shaking their jackets. 'No discussing the kidnap. Doctor's orders.'

He was on his way downtown to a jazz club called Hell's Kitchen. I'd called his friend, Marty, who plays alto sax when he isn't being cameraman for Angelworks.

'Guytalk!' I told him. 'Take Dad's mind off the whole Angel thing for me, *please*!'

So Dad went out as Connie and Zoey came in. Ziggy and Carter showed up five minutes later, after they'd called in at Marios on the corner of East Park Avenue and Twelfth Street for ice cream.

'Jeez, it's cold!' Ziggy blew into his hands after he handed me the tubs.

'It *is* ice cream,' I pointed out.

Zoey and Connie humoured me by laughing.

'Not that; the weather.' Ziggy acted hurt. 'Forget it. Here's me trying to make conversation, that's all.'

'Oh yeah, let's talk about the weather!' Connie giggled. 'That's why we asked you to join us!'

'Chocolate chip or blueberry?' Zoey cut in to save Zig's feelings.

If you want to know, my guess is that Ziggy and Zoey will be officially dating before too long.

Anyhow, with the weather talk and the ice cream, we didn't mention the 'A' word for ten whole minutes.

But then, 'I heard they arrested Angel's driver,' Ziggy mumbled, scooping out the tub of blueberry. 'Did anyone else get that, or am I the only one who watches TV round here?'

'Zig!' Zoey only comes up to his shoulder and she weighs 110 pounds, but she gave him a shove that knocked him sideways.

'Huh? Oh yeah, sorry, I forgot!'

I glanced at Carter, who was staring at the rug. I'd been doing pretty well, but suddenly I needed to talk the whole thing through with him. He wasn't interested, I guess. 'That's OK,' I told Zig, taking the empty tubs into the kitchen.

'It *could* be a joker with a weird sense of humour,' a

voice said behind my back. It was Carter. He'd closed the door so we had the room to ourselves.

I knew he was talking about our mystery surfer. Letting the tubs drop into the trash can, I turned to face him. 'Yeah, very funny. I'm laughing all the way.'

'You think this guy's for real?' Carter kept his distance. He followed every move I made, like I was under suspicion. Something to do with the frown line between his dark blue eyes, with the definite distance between him and me.

'Do you?' The fridge-freezer hummed in the corner as I turned the question around and waited for his answer.

'He's not an outsider. His last e-mail showed he knows too much about Stone's movements.' Carter had studied the second message and picked up the significant things.

'But is he for real?' I wanted more. 'Does he have Angel locked up somewhere, or is Stone the one?'

'I wouldn't put money on Stone,' was Carter's opinion as he leaned back against the door.

Then it burst open and a figure in a blue bomber jacket staggered through. Carter shot forward and stumbled against me, his shoulder smacking into my chest.

'Zig!' I yelled, pushing Carter off. Another split second and I realised the accident wasn't down to him.

He fell over backwards as another guy came after him. Zoey and Connie were giving little screams from the TV room. 'Oh, Jesus!' 'Oh, God!'

The unexpected visitor steadied himself against the sink. His leather jacket hung open, his dyed blond hair was grungy, his face filthy. By this time there seemed to be bodies all over the kitchen, including Carter, who had sprawled over Zig.

'Hey, Tommy.' I greeted Angel's ex as if this was a normal Saturday night social visit.

Tommy Jett had called at the house a couple of times in the past, looking for someone to go and drink with. I made out this was another of those situations. 'Dad's not here. He went down East Village.'

Carter and Ziggy were shaking from head to foot as they scraped themselves up from the floor. 'Jeez!' Ziggy breathed, like it was his last moment on this earth. He pinned himself back against the wall, praying to be beamed up.

'Wanna drink, Sean?' Tommy mumbled. His red eyes were little slits in a puffed up face. He swayed backwards and accidentally slammed up against the dishwasher.

He pressed buttons. Water swished and cascaded through the open door. The spray soaked Carter's T-shirt and dripped down his face.

'Dad isn't here, Tommy.' I repeated the sentence slowly. 'He went to Hell's Kitchen with Marty Applebaum.'

'. . . Yeah, on the rocks,' Tommy slurred. His slitty eyes took in Carter, who was fighting the dishwasher, and Ziggy, who was still trying to blend in with the wallpaper. 'Hey!' he said, suddenly straightening up. There was a glimmer of recognition.

'Uhh-oh!' Ziggy backed off towards the door.

'Shall I call the cops?' Zoey squeaked from the other room.

'Hey, you guys, wanna drink?' Tommy asked.

'Er, no.' Carter finally succeeded in slamming the dishwasher closed. He sat back against it, suds in his hair and up his nose. 'I think I'll take a rain check on that one, Tommy.'

And I started to laugh. It rose up my throat and came out of my nose like a snort, then exploded out of my mouth. I laughed until my stomach hurt.

'Yeah!' Carter got up and sulked wetly.

'Huh!' Ziggy peeled himself off the wall and squared his shoulders. 'Like, I thought he had it in for us.'

Connie and Zoey came in and paddled across the floor to see if I was OK.

'You guys wanna drink, or what?' Tommy was still offering. God knows how the poor guy had found Constitution Square, let alone number 18. The houses all look alike: traditional white fronts, six steps up to a pillared doorway.

'Black coffee!' I told him firmly, steering him to a chair, sitting him down at the table.

'You guys saved my life.' Half sober, Tommy's eyes filled with tears of gratitude. With a lot of help he remembered where he'd first met Zig and Carter: Circle train, Ginsberg Avenue, prior to the police cell.

'Aww!' Zig looked bashful.

I love Ziggy. One hundred and fifty pounds of bone and muscle, and nothing complicated about him.

'Can you believe the cops?' Tommy went on. He'd sieved a gallon of coffee between his teeth and relearned how to string sentences together. 'They're ready to throw the book at me over Angel – they only let me out when I put my hands on half a million dollars up front to pay my bail.

'I'm telling them I haven't seen her for weeks. She changed the locks at Heaven's Gate and gave her goons orders not to let me near the place.'

I glanced at Carter, then dropped in a quiet remark. 'Pam told them you called Wednesday morning.'

'Jeez,' he said equally low. Plenty of focus, a heavy emphasis on the one syllable.

'Why would she lie?' Carter risked a question, like going up to a bear in a cage and poking him gently through the bars. He was squeaky clean after his encounter with the dishwasher, his hair spiky, his T-shirt still damp. I felt a smile creeping up every time I looked at him.

'Ask the lady,' Tommy growled. 'You wanna know what I think? I think it's so long since Pam told it like it is, she don't know the difference any more. Lies, truth; it's all the same to her.'

'Yeah, but why would she want to point the finger directly at you?' I wanted a better answer.

'Easy.' It was Tommy's turn to treat me like the simpleton, speaking slow, spelling it out. 'She and Harvey Stone go way back . . .' He waited, looked around the table at me, Carter, Ziggy, Connie and Zoey.

'I thought it was *Rais* and Stone,' Connie whispered with a puzzled frown. 'Aren't they the ones who were an item?'

'O . . . Kay . . .' Tommy drawled while he tried to

think of a nice way to put it. 'Stone likes the ladies, see. He don't mind more than one girlfriend; he ain't particular about that. So Rais and Pam are both in the picture. Course, that can be a problem. It leads to arguments between the girls.'

'Yeah!' Connie and Zoey said they could appreciate that.

Tommy raised both hands so we could see his palms, like the conductor of an orchestra calling for attention. 'Get this. Rais is suddenly out of the picture, no fault of her own. Pam feels OK about this. Now Stone is all hers. The only problem is, Angel's missing and Rais is in the morgue. Someone has to take the rap. That someone had better not be Stone; that's the way Pam sees it.'

'So her lie about your visit puts the cops on the wrong track.' Zoey got it. Everyone got it, including Ziggy.

'But forensic find Stone's fingerprints all over the crime scene,' Zig said. 'You're out and he's in a cell; end of story.'

'So why didn't they clean up after them?' Connie's order-obsessed mind came out in the query. She backs her school books with colour co-ordinated paper and keeps an alphabetical file of the CDs she owns.

Tommy shrugged. The question hadn't occurred to him. Order wasn't his thing.

'OK, so let me get this straight.' (I'm sounding like Connie, I know.) I checked facts on an invisible list. 'Pam covered up for Stone. She may be involved up to her neck. The cops have got the right man this time, and pretty soon they'll find out from him where he's keeping Angel prisoner.'

Connie, Zoey and Ziggy nodded hard. Carter didn't, I noticed.

'Hey,' Tommy said as he got up ready to leave. He looked surprised that he could stand straight, put one foot firmly in front of another for a change. 'I never brought Angel into this.'

'Yes, but the guy who killed Rais must also be the one who abducted Angel!' I insisted. It was logical; anyone could see that. Even if the cops were holding Stone and the e-mails were still coming through, it was still possible that Harvey Stone was responsible. He could have staggered the messages and programmed them to come through at different times. Technically he could do this, I knew.

You see how much by this time I wanted it to be Stone.

Tommy shrugged again. 'You know how many death

threats Angel got last year?'

'What?' I stood up and followed him. 'What are you talking about?'

'Fifteen,' he went on, flicking me off as he headed for the front door. 'Fifteen people wanted to kill her; that's more than one a month.'

'Yeah, but . . . !' The door opened, snow whirled into the hallway. Tommy was out on the step in what looked like a blizzard.

'All I'm saying is, there are a lot of weirdos out there,' he said in a final kind of way, turning up his sheepskin collar and wandering into the Square in search of his next drink.

I closed the door and found Carter practically breathing down my neck.

'What kind of car does Angel have?' he asked.

Where did that question come from?

'White Mercedes,' I told him, staring deep into his blue eyes. The lashes are thick, there are flecks of light grey in amongst the dark blue. 'Why?'

8

'Mercedes to Hades'... 'Mercedes to Hades'. The guy's
sense of humour bugged me. I woke up early Sunday still
thinking about that part of the e-mail.

'Where's Hades?' I asked Marcie.

She wore Ocean's black T-shirt and her legs were bare,
her hair in small braids, mouth full of breakfast cereal.
'Ain't it upstate New York?'

'Yeah!' I smirked and gave up on my Mensa sister. 'You
heard of a place called Hades?' I asked Mom.

She leaned over and sniffed at my hair, recognised the
smell. 'Why did you wash it with detergent?'

'Don't ask. Concentrate. I need to know about this
place.'

'Hayseed?' She went out into the hallway with a stack
of clean laundry.

'Hades.' I raised my voice. 'H-A-D-E-S!'

'... Hell!' Damien yelled from his bedroom.

'Son, don't swear...' Mom began the tired old routine.
'It ain't nice. Your pop don't like to hear it.'

'Hades means hell!' My kid brother appeared in his door as I went and stood at the bottom of the stairway. Nine years old come May and he's way ahead of the rest of us. 'It's some old word from myths and legends. I looked it up on Encarta already.'

'Mercedes to Hell'? Yeah, thanks. Our surfing weirdo was telling us he was a bright guy. He knew stuff from Shakespeare and the myths. And he made sure his grammar was good.

I checked the e-mail from the One for Sorrow sender a hundred times. 'Mercedes to Hades. And where's that? Well, that's for you adoring fans to work out before Monday night . . .'

And now it was Sunday morning and I had the feeling that the cops were moving in hard on Harvey Stone and ignoring the rest. They worked logically, like Kate.

I let the idea of Kate interfere with my own thought process. This was enjoyable, until the uncalled for suspicion hit me that Kate and Ziggy were getting way too close. No, don't even think about it! Then Mom threw my jacket at me and told me to take Damien to the park.

I took one look out of the window. The street was white. Cars crawled along top-heavy with nine inches of white crust. 'It's snowing out there!'

'I know it.' She shoved a snowboard into my arms. 'Teach your kid brother a new sport.'

That's how come I was carrying the board up the hill in Fortune Park to the Constitution Monument at the top. With Damien and a thousand other kids. My legs were caked with freezing cold snow. This was *not* my idea of fun.

'I don't need you,' Damien was telling me. 'I can do this by myself.'

We reached the top and I gave him the board. He put it down in the snow and stood on it. Problem. He didn't move an inch. Other kids whooshed and whizzed by.

'Push yourself off by scooting one foot over the ground,' I advised. Snowflakes the size of goose feathers landed on my face.

'You push me!' he whined.

'Thought you said you didn't need me.' I gave him a starting shove.

'Who-oh-oah!' Damien's arms shot out to either side. He lasted five seconds then toppled.

I had to run down the hill and pick the kid up before someone crashed into him. 'Watch!' I said, sliding the board under my feet. Big shot big brother.

I lasted two seconds, maybe three.

Damien ploughed after me whooping and laughing. As he stooped to pull me up, snow slid from the peak of his baseball cap and landed on my head. 'My turn!' he yelled, charging with the board back up to the monument fence.

On his second attempt he stayed up until halfway down the hill. Third time, after he'd met up with kids from school, he could've been mistaken for a professional.

'Great!' I told him through chattering teeth. I was the abominable snowman out there, clumping about with ice hanging off my boots and snow in my hair.

Danny Kelly's dad took pity. He had leather gloves, woollen scarf, a cap with ear flaps. 'You run along home, Joey,' he said. 'I'll take care of Damien for you.'

It felt like a good deal to me. So I left the park to Damien and his mob of eight years old snowboarding whizzkids, trudging, slipping and sliding down the slope towards Constitution Square.

'A Mercedes to Hades' . . . Hades means Hell . . . Not that old thing! Give me a break! I was talking to myself like those guys who freeze to death at the South Pole. Man, this was serious.

'Carter?'

Kate was calling me from number 18. I ducked my chin inside my coat collar and walked on.

She ran down her steps to catch me up. 'OK, so ignore me!'

I turned round like I was surprised. This was set to ruin the look I got from her last night when she told me what make of car Stone drove Angel round in.

Last night we were getting on great. I was in with an even chance along with Ziggy. This morning I was the abominable snowman, complete with red nose.

'You must be freezing!' she said.

'Yeah.' *Shudder, shudder, chatter, chatter.*

'Come in!'

'No . . . thanks.'

'Yeah, really! I just called your house. I wanted to show you something!'

So, clump-clump, slide and skid up Kate's steps, kicking the snow off my boots, melting all over her hallway.

'Come through!' She took me to her dad's small office, off the main living-room. It was stuffed with TV monitors, sound systems, computers. 'Dad's working over at Heaven's Gate again,' she explained.

'On a Sunday?' *Drip-drip, sniff-sniff.* Gorgeous!

'Yeah. Imelda's sick with a migraine. He has to finalise stuff for next week's show.' Kate called me over to a computer screen. 'I can't stop thinking about the Angel thing. You know what Tommy said about the death threats?'

'Fifteen in one year.' As I dried out, I began to steam. My jacket smelled of damp camel.

'I asked Dad when he got back last night. He said, yeah; security around Angel had to be tight because of it. Imelda kept a file; a list of names who might be a problem if these people got near her. He said it happens when you're famous; it's one of the downsides.'

'OK.' I nodded. This was getting interesting. 'Did he show you the list?'

'Here, on this file.' Kate pointed to the screen. 'Imelda updates it every time a threat or a problem comes through.'

'What kind of problem?'

'Say Angel has a guest on the show who turns violent, like the bearded gorilla from last week. His name's near the bottom of the list, see. Someone to watch out for. But a lot of the names you can forget about, like this one.'

'Michael Harris.' I read the name and address. 'Oxford, England.'

'Eight of them live abroad,' Kate explained, 'so I guess we count them out. 'Three have prison addresses, so likewise.'

I frowned and got my head around this. Three guys in

gaol send Angel death threats. Like, that's really gonna get them early parole! There are a lot of weirdos out there, like Tommy said.

'Which only leaves us with five or six,' Kate went on. She pointed with her index finger. The finger tapered away to a rounded pink nail, smooth and a little bit shiny, with a white crescent at the very tip. Yeah, I know – I was into details I wouldn't normally pick up. 'Joseph J. Godin . . . Marilyn Molko . . . Keith Recile . . . Brett Roberts . . .'

The fingernail tapped the glass. 'No address,' she noted.

I couldn't see her face for the screen of black hair. How can human hair be so long, straight and glossy?

'Carter?'

'Yeah, no address.'

'Brett Roberts is the other guy from the "Love Cheats" show, the one who walked out.'

My brain wasn't connecting like it should. Brett Roberts: thin, nervy guy with straight, heavy eyebrows, very upset.

'He's on Imelda's list!' Kate turned to look at me, eyes flashing impatient sparks. 'C'mon, Joey; you're the one with the hunches. Roberts storms out of the studio like he hates the whole world, but especially Angel Christian. She's made him look like an idiot in front of twelve million people!'

'Got it!'

You've never seen brown like the brown of Kate Brennan's eyes. Streaked like the shells of hazelnuts, flecked with amber; they're amazing.

The dark hair swung back across her face as she turned to the computer, pressed keys and came up with another list. 'Brett Roberts' cheating girlfriend is called Anita Schiff,' she told me. 'The Angelworks researchers came across her waiting tables in Marytown. They made a file on her before she came on the show. See, this is her address.'

584 Sixteenth Street was a tenement stuck between a parking lot and a downmarket sale room specialising in bathroom fixtures. There was a burnt-out car at the foot of the steps, all kinds of garbage spilling over the sidewalk. I stepped over a kid's cycle half-hidden under the snow, and warned Kate to take care.

I was reading the names against the buzzers – Simpson . . . Basement, Freed . . . Ground, Goldsboro . . . 1A – when a kid opened the door and shot out as we stepped in. The door banged shut behind us.

'Yuck!' Kate looked round at peeling yellow walls and a stone stairway that spiralled up a central well. Ten floors up, there was a big skylight covered in snow, leaving the whole place gloomy and feeling like it was underwater. 'What number do we want?'

'I didn't get to Schiff,' I admitted. I already had a trapped-in-the-Titanic-after-it-hit-the-iceberg feeling.

'Schiff?' A woman aged about ninety poked her head out of the door marked Freed. The little hair she had was twisted on top of her head like a thin grey rope, she was minus her teeth and weighed less than a hundred and ten. I guess she spent the whole of what was left of her life snooping on callers. 'You want Schiff?'

'Anita.' Kate swallowed hard. 'Do you know her?'

'3C.' The crone squeaked then slammed her door.

Kate glanced at me. 'I guess we must look OK.'

'Either that, or she hates her neighbours enough to tell even a mass murderer where Anita lives.'

'I heard that!' Mrs Freed croaked through her mailbox.

'Some security system!' I kidded.

Kate and I took the stairs two at a time to the third storey. A stone landing contained doors to four apartments; 3C was to the right. Without stopping to think, we went straight ahead and buzzed.

For ages nothing happened. We thought Anita Schiff must be out.

'At church,' I said. Another bad joke.

Then, after we pressed the buzzer some more, we heard signs of life.

The door opened. A head appeared. 'Yeah?'

I heard Kate gasp.

We had in mind Anita Schiff of the 'Love Cheats' show. Blonde hair puffed up and falling over her bare shoulders, inches of make-up, ready to make a pass at anything that moved.

This woman wore a towelling bathrobe that may once have been white. Her hair was like straw straggling over her face. OK so far? Now, it's beam me up time.

The face looked like every feature had been unlovingly rearranged.

A cut on the mouth had swollen the bottom lip and dried into a black mark that ran all the way down her chin. One cheek was puffed up and bruised purple. There was another cut across the left eyebrow, or the place where an eyebrow should be. I guess Anita plucked them bare, ready to paint them on again in a shape she preferred. The eyebrow cut was more of a gash that wouldn't close; no flesh on the bone there to help it heal, so the wound was still weeping pus.

To cut it short, Anita was now a candidate for the Violence Against Women slot that Angel had planned before she disappeared.

'Who did this?' I heard Kate gasp.

Anita put a cigarette to her mouth with a trembling hand. 'Who wants to know?'

'I'm Kate Brennan. This is Joey Carter. My dad produces 'Angel'. Can we come in?'

'No.' Anita stared at us with dead eyes. 'Look, I'm busy, OK.'

'Hold it.' Kate stuck her foot in the door before it closed. 'It's Brett we want. Is he here?'

'No.' Cigarette smoke drifted through the crack. Anita pushed hard against Kate's foot.

'Do you know where he is?'

'No. Not here. Now get lost.'

I leaned on the door to help Kate. 'You want to get Brett locked up for what he did to you?' I asked quietly.

The pressure on the door eased. Anita let us half-fall into the hall. Inside, the apartment was completely trashed. Mirrors were broken, chairs smashed, drapes ripped down from the windows.

'Yeah,' she said with a long sigh, then took another pull on her cigarette.

'Just tell us where he is and we'll be out of here,' I promised.

'I don't know where he went after he left here.' Anita glazed over as she took in the wreckage. 'All I know is he was out of control after the show. He got home before me and trashed the place, then when I showed up, he started on me.'

I stared at the damage on Anita's face. This is what you get if you sleep with your boyfriend's brother. Twenty eight times, for God's sake. I'm not saying Brett Roberts was right to do what he did. I'm saying you can understand how it happened.

'Where would he stay?' Kate asked. 'After he beat you up, where would he go?'

Not to his brother's place, that's for sure.

'Look, I have no idea!' Anita started to tug at her hair, to try and hide her bruises. She lit another cigarette with shaking hands. 'All I know is, he went crazy.'

'Would he go in to work?' Kate persisted. She'd kept her head through all this.

'Maybe. How should I know? I haven't been out of the door since it happened.'

'Where does he work?'

'Lots of different places. Clubs, bars in East Village.'

'What does he do?'

It was hard to see Anita through the fierce cloud of fresh blue smoke. 'Musician,' she muttered. Then, with an ironic laugh: 'Guys like Brett are the sensitive type. Artists, writers . . . they're all the same. Uptight. Crazy . . .'

'Let's go,' I whispered to Kate. We'd got all we could out of Anita. I wasn't ready to admit it, but my stomach was queasy. I found it too easy to picture mirrors smashing, cuts bleeding . . . And the smoke was making me nauseous.

We went downstairs to the Titanic lobby.

'He plays the clubs in East Village!' Kate hung on to the shreds of information we'd gained. Not much, but something.

I fumbled with the door lock, desperate to get out into the cold air.

'Try Sonny Boy's on Thirty-third!' a voice croaked through the mailbox: Mrs Freed, Superspy. 'Or the Blues Bar on East Grand Street, or Southern Comfort on Jackson Plaza. If he's not there, try Hell's Kitchen on the corner of Ninth Avenue!'

9

'One for Sorrow 3. Sunday, February 19th, midday.'

Carter and I arrived back at my place to another e-mail. I went on line as soon as we got there, while Joey called home to check on Damien. Something must have told me that the kidnapper would want to keep us guessing.

'Yes, folks, the Sands of Time are trickling through the Egg-timer of Destiny faster than you think! Thirty six hours to go, then Angel finds her rightful place among the stars.

'Not the fake kind of TV and movie stars you see in the trashy gossip pages. I'm talking heavenly bodies, the real thing. This is Day 2 of the countdown. Two for Joy! Angel's beautiful eyes are bright with tears. She's so happy . . . *we're* so happy, we could die!'

'Is that it?' Carter came off the phone and read the e-mail.

'Isn't it enough?' I snapped back. 'He's only threatening to kill Angel in thirty six hours' time!'

Carter took a step back and put his head on one side. 'Sorry. You're right. I mean, how come he can't just ask for a ransom like anyone else?'

Obviously we both wanted the e-mailer to play it straight and ask for millions of Angel's dollars, thus proving his sanity.

And now, when I said 'he', I definitely had in mind Brett Roberts.

Not that Carter and I would find it easy to convince anyone else of this theory. After all, they hadn't been to Sixteenth Street and seen what had happened to Anita Schiff's face. Not even the cops, since they'd been so busy trying to pin the thing on Tommy.

We were staring so hard at the screen, lost in our own thoughts, that when the phone rang, we both jumped a mile. I picked it up and listened.

'Hi, honey!'

'Hi, Dad.' I guessed he was checking up on me.

'You had some lunch?'

'Not yet. Carter's here.' For some reason, I held back from explaining where we'd been. I did tell him there was another crazy e-mail on Angel's website.

'Yeah, I saw it. I spoke to the cops about it.'

'How come?' Taking the phone to the office window, I looked out on a white, Christmas card world. The snow lay on the roofs like a layer of sugar-icing; the flakes kept on drifting down.

'Sergeant Fiegel called to run through Wednesday's events with me – again!' Dad sounded tired beneath the cheerful front, and a little bit edgy.

'So what did he say about the e-mails?'

'They think it's a weirdo who's wasting their time . . . well, I won't repeat his exact words. Let's just say the cops have put a guy on to it, but they don't take it too seriously. It's Stone's prints and his complicated love life that are taking centre stage down at FCPD.'

My heart sank. If Dad couldn't make the cops broaden out their investigation, what chance did Carter and I have of persuading anybody? 'Did they talk to Pam yet?' I asked, thinking that the answer had to be yes. No way could even these dumb cops leave Angel's scary stepsister out of the picture much longer.

'Nope.' There was a long pause, a couple of clicks on the line, then Dad's voice came back sounding kind of strange. 'Honey, I gotta go!'

'When will you be home?'

'Late. Listen, you said you might drop by?'

'No . . . I never mentioned . . .'

He broke in sharply with, 'Well, call a rain check, will you? I'm real busy. Bye!'

'He's more tired than I thought.' I told Carter what he'd said, then frowned and bit my bottom lip. 'I sure wish he'd take a break.'

'How about we ignore orders and go over there to persuade him?'

Carter's suggestion, delivered with perfect timing, seemed like a good idea. 'With these!' I grabbed a bag of Dad's favourite cookies from the kitchen shelf. 'We can walk across the park and be there in half an hour!'

So, in spite of Dad's warning, me and Carter trudged knee-deep through the snow, dodging the snowboarders, me clutching the choc chip cookies, Carter thinking aloud.

'If Mrs Dinosaur-Features Freed is right about Brett Roberts' places of work, my guess is he plays jazz,' he said to the dirty stone face of Benjamin Franklin.

Carter was staring up at the statue perched on top of the column on Monument Hill. The statue's three-cornered hat was laden with snow, the eyes cold and blank.

(*Why was Dad acting strange? What had happened during the long pause when the phone line clicked? Had a person walked into the room and said something to upset him?*)

'Which means, even though we never heard of him, he must be pretty well known to jazz lovers in the town; like, to geriatrics over the age of fifty. And maybe to musicians in general.'

(*Dad was working alone today. Imelda had a migraine. Who could have walked in on our conversation?*)

Carter walked along, hands in his jacket pockets, collar turned up. 'I'll ask Marcie. Maybe someone in her band knows which club Brett Roberts is playing right now.'

(*Dad never cut me dead like that. Why had he been so clear about me not calling at Heaven's Gate? Something was wrong here . . .*)

We reached the far side of the park and crossed the highway on to West Park Avenue. The traffic crawled through the snow, some drivers had pulled up on the hard shoulder to stare at the gang of journalists gathered like vultures around Angel's place.

'. . . Kate?'

'Huh?'

'I said, your dad could ask his friend, Marty Applebaum, about Brett Roberts.'

'Sure, good idea.' (*Something was definitely not right.*)

I frowned as I pushed past a couple of journalists and went up to the cop on duty to show her a special visitors' pass which Dad had given me to get in and out of the Angelworks section of the building. This was the part of the house overlooking a side lawn, facing Harvey Stone's lodge.

The cop checked the pass. She looked bored and cold. 'Go ahead,' she muttered.

'Hey, who are you?' the journalists yelled, jostling for position to get a good shot, in case we turned out to be someone important.

'We're nobody,' Carter told them, following me through.

I glanced across the smooth, white lawn towards the garage where Angel's car was normally kept. The door was open, the garage empty. Then I looked ahead at the house. A light was on in the office room where I knew Dad would be working. Reaching the door and still clutching my bag of cookies, I punched in some numbers on the security panel and walked in ahead of Carter.

Something told me not to call out Dad's name. There was a corridor with small rooms off, leading to the main Angelworks office at the end. This was where the light was on. I could hear the faint hum of computers and then a sudden, sharp ring of a phone, cut off quickly by a recorded message. 'We're sorry we can't take your call . . .'

So where was he? My whole body went tense as my heartbeat quickened. This was weird; everything was too quiet, too dead.

Carter sensed I was scared and went ahead down the corridor, looking into rooms to left and right. He came to the main office and stopped short, putting his arm across the doorway, like you would if you wanted to stop someone getting by.

I started to run; maybe for only four or five seconds until I caught up with him, but it felt longer. The corridor started to tilt and grow narrow, the dark blue carpet seemed to rise up, the ceiling to come down and try to crush me. 'What is it? What happened?'

'Don't go in!' Carter's arm barred my way.

I ducked beneath it, lost my balance and half crawled into the office.

There were a hundred sheets of paper cascading from a tray on the desk, an overturned chair, a glass lamp smashed on to the floor. The white paper had spread across more blue carpet. It was stained crimson.

'Blood!' I couldn't breathe. My heart was about to break through my ribcage, it knocked so loud.

'Hold it. Get the cops!' Carter grabbed me and pushed me towards the door.

The blood looked like paint splashed and smeared

across the paper, like a mad artist had been at work. I was nauseous, I was faint at the sight of it. I dropped to my knees and scrabbled for the nearest sheet. It was wet and sticky. I stared at my fingertips. They glistened bright red.

'Get the cops!' Carter shouted.

The phone rang again. 'We're sorry we can't take your call . . .'

The door slammed behind us. Pam Collins stepped out.

'Where's Dad? What have you done?' I didn't care that she was holding a knife, I just ran at her until Carter pulled me back.

He swung me round behind him, watched and waited.

'. . . Please leave a message and we'll get back to you as soon as we can.'

'It's very simple,' Pam said, leading us through a door that led into the residential part of the house. A trail of blood ran the length of a beige carpet; small spatters, not the smears and splashes we'd seen in the office. 'If you can get Sean to change his story, we call the paramedics. If not, he bleeds to death.'

Dad was lying on the floor in a room with a bed, a

chest of drawers, a TV. The drapes were drawn, but an open slit cast a slim wedge of daylight across his bleeding body.

I was kneeling beside him, cradling his head in my arms.

'Tell him the deal.' Pam ordered Carter to repeat the terms she'd just explained to us. She gestured with the knife which she held in her left hand. It was long and pointed, glistening with blood.

Carter took off his jacket, rolled it up ready to hand to me so I could press it against Dad's side to stem the flow of blood.

'Not yet!' Pam moved between us, slashing the knife into the soft fabric of the jacket. Her face was like a mask, her eyes unblinking. She looked down at my dad as if he was an object. 'Tell him first. Make him understand.'

Carter didn't take his eyes off Pam. He backed off, took a deep breath, began. 'Sean, she wants you to go back to the cops and give them a different story about what happened last Thursday morning. The new version includes Stone helping you to break into Rais's room.'

Dad looked up at me with helpless, confused eyes.

'Hush!' I whispered, stroking his forehead.

'You have to say you got here at eleven, looking for

98

Angel, and you found both Stone and Pam looking at the stain in the ceiling. You all three went upstairs together. You and Stone broke down the door, you all went in and found the maid stabbed.'

I'll never know how Carter stayed calm just then. I was falling apart, looking into my dad's eyes as he begged silently for us to help him.

'That way, there's a good reason to find Stone's fingerprints all over the room. The cops won't have anything on him and they'll have to let him go.'

Dad closed his eyes and a big shudder shook his whole body.

'Stay awake!' I cried. 'Tell her yes, then we can call an ambulance!'

Crazy. Completely crazy. You could see it in her green eyes, blank and cold as the statue in the park.

'Tell her yes.' Carter backed me up.

We both knew that it had gone way past reason into the wild logic of a maniac desperate to save the man she loved. 'Say it's a deal, Sean,' Pam coaxed. 'Don't argue with me any more.'

Dad struggled to keep his eyes open. 'OK!'

Pam nodded and let Carter hand the jacket to me. I pressed it hard against the gash in Dad's side, just beneath the ribcage on the right hand side. Please God, don't let him lose any more blood!

'Call the ER!' I pleaded. 'Get an ambulance here quick!'

'. . . We're sorry we can't take your call . . .' The machine aborted another attempt to get through to Angelworks.

Carter had left me in the bedroom with Dad and Pam. He'd burst through doors, run back into the office, from where I could hear the faint, apologetic voice still echoing. Pam was looking at the blade in a puzzled way, as if she didn't know how it had got there. Then she stared at me pressing the pad of Carter's jacket hard against Dad's side.

'. . . Hold it!'

'Easy! Don't move!'

The room was suddenly full of cops pointing guns. The black metal barrels were trained on Pam.

She dropped the knife on to the soft cream carpet.

Then the paramedics came in in their zip-up suits and surgical gloves, carrying an oxygen mask, resuscitation equipment, body supports, a stretcher.

They had to lift me away from my dad and carry me out of there, put me in the ambulance with him and race across town to Fortune City General.

10

The cops were waiting outside the door. You have to understand; it was Sergeant Fiegel on the phone, trying to get through to Pam to fix up a time for her to go down and see him at the Police Department. He'd finally decided it was time to make a move.

When he got the message machine three times, knowing that Sean hadn't left the building yet, he concluded something was wrong and sent in his men.

They arrived at the same time Pam Collins sent me through to the office to call the hospital. I could open the door for them. No magic involved. No heroics. Just luck.

If you could call it that, with Sean hooked up to machines in the ER and Kate sitting by his bed looking so pale it was like she was the one who had lost all the blood.

Pam was in an interview room downtown, telling Fiegel how come it had been necessary for her to stab both Rais and Sean, I guess.

Rais because she kept getting in the way between

her and Stone. Three's a crowd.

Sean because . . . well, we'd get the full story from him after the sedation wore off and they'd run the tests on his internal organs to check that the knife hadn't sliced through anything too important.

The way I saw it, Pam had broken into his phone call to Kate and put pressure on him to let Stone off the hook. Maybe it was something she'd been trying all day.

Maybe then she'd flipped and come in with the knife, Sean had tried to get some kind of warning through to Kate by saying what he did, we'd set off across the park with the cookies, and arrived after a fight, which Sean had lost pretty conclusively. Pam is tall and strong, remember. She's also obsessed. And she was the one with the knife.

By that time she'd lost it completely. But who knows for how long she'd been on the brink? Maybe it was years since she'd seen life the way most of the rest of us see it. Living in Angel's shadow was a hard act. Being invisible, being the Woman the World Forgot, maybe you invent a different set of rules which includes it being OK to let people bleed to death if they don't do what you want.

Don't ask me.

All I know is she was marched out of Heaven's Gate at

gunpoint. A hundred cameras flashed, caught a huddled figure shrouded by a blanket. The cops pushed her roughly into a car, turned on their blue lights and vanished her.

Heading through the ER lobby to get a breath of air thirty minutes after I'd arrived at the hospital, I heard Fiegel updating another cop. His grey hair had a ridge where his cap fitted too tight around his head. The cap was under his arm now, he was closing his eyes and tugging at his moustache like he was tired.

'The doc says Brennan will make it. There's a small tear in the intestine which they can sew up pretty good. The guy was lucky; it's mostly flesh wound.'

'What did they get from the Collins woman?' the other cop asked. I recognised her as the one on duty at Heaven's Gate when we arrived.

'It turns out she's Angel Christian's stepsister.'

'I never knew that!'

'She's got a grudge, big time! But from what I hear, she's coming clean over the maid.'

The female cop made a noise between 'Huh!' and 'Yeah!', meaning, 'You'd be a fool to believe *that*.' 'I still got Stone down for that,' she said.

And personally, I agreed with her. I don't think Pam knew what the hell was happening until later.

'So Collins is covering up for the boyfriend?'

She nodded. 'Who cares? For me, they can both go down.'

Just then, the doors flew open and three stretchers raced by. Nurses ran into the lobby, paramedics wheeling the trolleys yelled names, ages, BP numbers. I stepped out of the way, and when it was over, the two cops had gone.

'Kate, you should come home with us,' Mom told her gently.

She'd arrived to pick me up from the hospital at five-thirty. She said no way should Kate go home to an empty house.

'That's OK. My mom's flying in from New York.' Kate sounded a million miles away, still staring at her dad lying asleep beyond a glass partition, with nurses, charts, tubes, screens all around him.

'Then come to our place until she gets here,' Mom insisted. 'Or let Joey wait with you at yours.'

Kate chose the second option, which was how come I found myself cooking frozen pizza in the microwave, then reading 'Not suitable for microwave cooking' on the box.

I can't tell you how bad it looked. It was a multi-coloured, oozing, biological disaster.

Kate laughed at me and threw the pizza in the garbage can. As soon as she stopped laughing, she sighed.

'Joey . . .' She looked at me with scared, dark eyes.

'I know.' I would've reached out and said it was fine, I was there, everything was gonna be OK. Kate would've let me hold her, if her Mom hadn't chosen that second to walk in on us.

'Would you believe, snow held up my plane by two whole hours!' she wailed, flinging her bag on the table, pausing for a nano-second to throw me a look that said, 'Get out of here!'

I didn't argue. I hit the exit and went right on home. But I didn't sleep, knowing I'd been that close — like inches — from a deep clinch with Kate Brennan.

Kate's mom gave me that look and stuck a label on me. The label said 'Blue collar', meaning, 'Not good enough for my daughter'. I would most likely end up working on a car assembly line with dirt under my fingernails. Forget the myth of all men being born equal, Benjamin bro. This is the real America.

Melissa Brennan was not to know that building cars is not my life's major ambition.

I let her step in to take care of her daughter, went home like I said, browsed the internet on Damien's computer. There were no more e-mails after the 'heavenly bodies' and 'Sands of Time' one, so I went to bed early.

When I woke next morning, after a heap of Mercedes to Hades nightmares, Damien was jumping on my bed.

'Beat it!' I threw him off, pulled the quilt over my head.

'Joey, school's closed 'cos of the snow!'

I sat up then. 'Yours or mine?' The schools were on the same campus, to the north of the town.

'Both! The heating gave out. Take me to the park snowboarding again, hey? Go on, take me!'

'I'm busy. Ask Marcie.' The nightmares included a white car driving over a cliff edge, falling hundreds of feet into a flaming pit. Bits of car fell off as it bounced against the rock – wheels and mirrors. The trunk flew open; a body fell out. Then the whole thing was swallowed by fire.

I tossed Damien off the bed again and got dressed. He went snowboarding with Danny Kelly while I took over his computer. Mercedes to Hades. Hades means Hell . . . I had to stop this taking over my life. If the cops had Stone and Pam for Rais's murder, didn't that mean the whole thing was over?

Anyway, I logged on to the Angelworks website. Take scenario number one: Stone and Pam stabbed the maid

106

between them and planned to get rid of what they thought was a dead body. That could have been any time before eleven a.m. on Thursday, when Sean arrived. Meanwhile, Angel walks in on them.

Crazy Woman Collins, who, as we all know, hates her stepsister, sees it as the best chance she's ever gonna have to turn things around and make Angel the Invisible Woman. She persuades Stone it's a great idea, and anyway, he's already in it up to his neck.

They kidnap Angel and start playing this crazy One for Sorrow game. Which leaves me thinking two things. One: they killed Angel the second she walked in on them and Rais. They dumped the body and the whole e-mail thing is a couple of psychos' idea of a good time.

Or two: they really do have Angel trapped somewhere, tormenting her before they kill her. And now they're locked up themselves in police cells and Angel is still a prisoner in an unknown location, about to starve or suffocate, whatever.

Really, Sergeant Fiegel and his colleagues had better work fast on that one.

Or else, there was Scenario Number Two, and it involved Brett Roberts. I read this morning's e-mails from people who had spotted Angel in New Mexico and Toronto, and from a guy in Idaho who told us not to worry; he'd had a vision, and Angel was safe in heaven with Elvis, John Lennon and Kurt Cobain.

'One for Sorrow 4. Monday, February 20th, 8.30 a.m.,' I read on the screen. 'Really, you guys out there are very slow. I'm disappointed. I thought we'd have more fun.

'Fifteen and a half hours to lift-off. Picture it: Ten, Nine, Eight . . . Three, Two, One! There's a tankful of fuel in this rocket, honey. Pity about the smell. Gasoline isn't Angel's favourite perfume, as it turns out.

'When I spread it generously around the leather upholstery, she begged me not to. I said I needed to be prepared for the countdown, but that we still had plenty of opportunity to talk and say our goodbyes.

'The sweet thing is, Angel just offered me all her money again; everything she owns if I spare her life.

'Who does this remind you of? Sad old Doctor Faustus and "I'll burn my books!" The problem is, the deal doesn't work if you already sold your soul. It took me some time to explain that to Angel.

'Anyway, I guess she may have a last message for her friends. Only time will tell.'

Half an hour later, Kate showed up.

'Mom's at the hospital,' she told me.

'How's your dad?'

'Doing great until Mom got there.' She gave me a pale smile. 'No, really, they say he's gonna make it.'

'Did you see this?' I showed her the latest message. I hadn't looked at it for thirty seconds, and when I did, I made a new connection. Call it lateral thinking, or just plain crazy. 'Hades is Hell. Brett Roberts plays jazz at Hell's Kitchen!'

I couldn't believe I hadn't thought of it sooner.

'The corner of Ninth Avenue!' Kate was there with me, a sudden flush on her face, an intake of breath before she spoke. 'C'mon, let's go!'

11

Carter and I took the Circle train to East Village. We looked down on a city clogged with dirty snow. It was banked to the sides of the black, shiny roads where ploughs had dumped it, spilling on to the sidewalks which had frozen overnight and turned into lumpy, ice-caked channels.

Neon signs lit up the windows of bakeries and delis, but no one with any sense was buying food on the kind of day when it was better to stay home and, come supper time, raid the deep freeze.

'Ninth Avenue!' the driver yelled, grinding to a halt. As he pushed a button, the doors slid open and introduced a blast of cold air.

The two other passengers in the carriage grumbled to each other about the weather. We got off fast, heard the doors close behind us and the train move off.

'OK, Einstein, what now?' I leaned over the rail and looked down the empty street. Coloured lights threaded through the bare branches of an avenue of trees were still lit, even though it was day. A car engine throbbed at the kerbside next to a news-stand. Behind, the stand, a flashing red sign spelled out the words 'Hell's Kitchen' in a flowing neon scrawl.

Carter took the metal steps down to the sidewalk two at a time. His breath came out as clouds of steam, drifting up towards me as I followed. 'We're looking for a white Mercedes,' he told me. 'It's here somewhere.'

Don't ask me why, but I believed him. 'What do we do when we find it?' I wanted to know.

He was busy peering through the window of the basement jazz club. Inside it was dark. There was row after row of empty tables with upturned chairs stacked on them; ten thirty on a Monday morning and pretty damn obviously closed. There was a 'Personnel Wanted' ad stuck crooked in one corner of the door. 'First we find it,' he insisted.

'Wha-d'ya-wan?' the old guy at the news-stand barked at us from across the sidewalk. He was dressed in an old, army-style greatcoat with tabs on the shoulders and shiny silver buttons. His fingers had on those half-gloves that left his grimy fingertips bare to handle small change.

'We're looking for a position waiting tables,' I lied. Pretty smart thinking.

'Service door, down the side alley.' The newspaper vendor gathered phlegm in his throat, coughed, then spat. It looked like he didn't think we had much chance of a job.

Carter nodded at me to take the advice anyway. So I backed up the steps to the street and picked my way along the icy sidewalk to the corner where Ninth crosses Twelfth Street. We turned into Twelfth, went fifty feet to the end of the tall, brick building, then came to what the vendor meant by 'side alley'.

It was the kind of passageway between two blocks where daylight never falls. Ten feet wide, if that, with blocked gutters and dirty walls rising fifteen, twenty floors and blocking out the sky. The walls had small, filthy windows here and there.

At ground level there was a series of big service doors; the metal type which rolls upwards and out of sight on some kind of pulley system. These doors bore a tattered patchwork of graffiti and old bills: 'Tonite Sonny Hayes and the Gingerbread Boys', 'Live Music, Old Grey Whistle Stop, Fridays', 'Cancelled', 'Post No Bills!'

'How far do we go?' I asked Carter. Stepping in

something soft in the gutter had just made me squirm. What could be soft and bright yellow under a layer of brown snow, for God's sake?

'A car could get down here,' he insisted, pointing to a small yard at the end of the alley. 'Let's take a look.'

'Wha–d'ya–wan?' A door opened and a short black guy in a leather coat gave us the neighbourhood greeting.

'Hell's Kitchen service door,' I shot back.

'You wanna wait tables?'

'Sure.' I met his suspicious gaze, drew his attention from Carter, who had gone on ahead.

'You old enough?'

'You the Personnel guy?' I asked.

He laughed and shrugged. 'You want Jasper Guziak, third door on your left.'

'Third on the left!' Quickly I caught up with Carter and pointed out a narrow black door. I glanced back down the alley to see the guy in the leather coat turn out on to Twelfth Street and leave us alone with the graffiti.

'Yeah, but let's take a look in the yard.'

Carter's not the pushover some guys think. He can be real single-minded.

He ignored the black door and picked his way through garbage bins to a square of concrete about twenty feet by fifteen, walls to all four sides, a service entrance into the back of Ninth Avenue on the left. We took our time to work out that we'd doubled back and come way past Hell's Kitchen. All the same, the yard was most likely shared by all the clubs and shops on the row.

'So?' I didn't like being down here. There was only one way in and one way out. It made me feel trapped. Squinting up towards the patch of murky grey daylight, I felt a splash of icy water hit my forehead and trickle down my face.

'So we try the door.' Carter stooped to ease his fingers under its multi-coloured, graffitied surface.

He pulled upwards but nothing shifted. So he stopped, went down on his hands and knees, sniffed at the two inch gap under the door.

'What?' I asked, hating the way he went quiet and stopped telling me what was going on.

'Gasoline!'

'So?' So, this was a gasoline store with cans stacked up to the ceiling, or maybe there was a junky old car in there with a leak from the gas tank. Or even, God forbid, Carter was wrong about the smell.

He jumped up and looked back down the alley, starting out of his skin when a cat poked its nose out of a trash can, heaved itself over the rim and slunk off up a metal staircase. 'The e-mailer told us about the gas, remember!'

I felt my eyes come out on stalks as I stared at the door and picked out a giant, red, 3-D message sprayed over all the other stuff on the door. It said 'Welcome to the Underworld!'

The words slid up as I read them. God, not again; the world had started to shift and tilt, like in the Angelworks corridor.

But no; this was real. The door was sliding out of sight, a square, black hole was opening up, the stink of gasoline belched out.

'Finally!' a voice said, like there was a huge joke that I didn't get.

I grabbed at Carter's arm as a guy stepped out into the yard. The face was chalk-white above a shabby black overcoat buttoned to the neck, the eyebrows heavy. 'So someone out there has a brain after all!' Roberts said with a twisted smile. 'It makes life *so* much more interesting.'

I turned to run, dragging Carter with me.

Roberts moved fast and beat me to the metal fire escape which the cat had climbed. He swung a punch, caught me on my cheek, sent me crashing against the sharp edge of the bottom step.

We were inside the garage. The door was closed. My cheek was throbbing with a dull pain and I was gagging from the stench of gasoline.

Carter had taken a few punches as I lay sprawled on the metal step. I could see a small cut above his left eye, a tear at the corner of his mouth.

The way I could see this was that, after he'd kicked and punched us back into the yard and under the raised door, Roberts had turned on the car ignition and switched the headlights full on. The beams bounced off a brick wall and shed as much light as we could want.

We were in a room just big enough to take the Mercedes, but with a high roof supported by metal beams. The walls were cold and damp, covered in an ancient layer of bubbling, peeling paint; once white, now the colour of the soiled snow outside.

So the polished, gleaming limousine looked all the more pristine white, the red leather of its interior soft and luxurious. But the leather was stained and spoiled by gasoline, the smell worst of all from the back seat where the empty can lay with its screw-top missing.

'Where's Angel?' Carter muttered. 'What did you do with her?'

Roberts had locked the garage door. Now he slid into the driver's seat, turning the wheel and swaying like he was taking a sharp corner fast. He made a screeching noise of tyres burning the road. 'Look in the trunk,' he recommended. Like he was reading a menu and suggesting a main course: '*Try the alligator steak. It's very, very good*!'

'It's locked!' I slammed the lid of the trunk in a frenzy. My face was wet with sweat, my heart pumping adrenalin like crazy.

Roberts killed the lights. We were in total darkness. He started to hum and tap the steering wheel.

' "*Well, it's one for the money,*
Two for the show,
Three to get ready
Now go, cat, go!" '

I felt myself start to cry. It shook through me, from right under the centre of my ribs, a rising, choking sob.

'Open it!' Carter yelled. His voice bounced off the walls.

There was a series of dull thuds from inside the trunk; one kick, two, three.

Angel was alive.

'Open it!' Carter screamed at Roberts.

' "*Blue, blue . . . blue suede shoes,*
Blue, blue . . . blue suede shoes . . .
You can do anythin'
But lay off of my blue suede shoes!" '

12

Welcome to the Underworld, welcome to Hell.

Stuck in a back-lot garage with a madman and a TV star. The TV star was tied up in the trunk. We were all set to go up in flames and burn, baby, burn.

Roberts sang his song, then turned the lights back on.

'Let me introduce myself,' he grooved to Kate and me, stepping out of the limo with a twisted, show-businessy grin.

'We know who you are,' she gasped between sobs.

Me, I wouldn't have given him that much.

The thumps from inside the trunk had stopped. Picture it: being locked up in a dark metal box for three days, then hearing voices. *Save me. Deliver me from Evil.*

But how? The guy was sitting on a half million dollar, chrome-plated, leather-upholstered fire-bomb.

'So who am I?' Roberts challenged, moving in too close to Kate and breathing over her.

She tried to push him off, but he pinned her into the scummy corner. She went down and I rushed to help her up out of the oily puddle seeping in under the door.

'So who are *you*?' He acted like he hadn't touched her; back to the charm offensive. How d'you do? Pleased to meet you. Very schmaltzy.

But when neither of us gave him an answer, back came the psycho on speed. This time, both Kate and me were slammed against the car, then down in the puddle. There was new thumping from inside the trunk.

'She's upset,' Roberts told us. 'You upset her!'

'Please let her out!' Kate begged. She'd gone beyond those dry, choking sobs into a kind of little-girl pleading voice.

'Why, sure!' The crazy bastard turned on the grin. He went and punched a button on the dash. The lid of the trunk clicked and sprang up a fraction of an inch. 'Open it!' he told me.

I put my fingers under the cold metal rim and lifted the lid. Angel was in there, gagged and blindfolded, ankles tied with thick blue rope, hands bound behind her back. She lay on her side in black trousers and a creased cream sweater, legs curled up towards her chest, so still you'd have said she was dead.

It was like a hare caught in a headlight beam; he freezes out of terror and then you run him down.

'Oh God!' Kate groaned.

'Hey, she's fine!' Roberts insisted, coming to lean over the trunk. 'Come and look; she's still breathing.'

'Stop it!' Kate again.

I said nothing, looking round the lousy place for a way out. No chance. The walls were solid brick, the door we'd come through was locked.

'So, if you know who I am, then you know why we're here.' Crazy Brett was wrenching off Angel's blindfold and gag, taking a long bladed knife from his suede leather jacket and cutting through the ropes. In fact, he was setting her free. But she still lay there on her side, staring out at us like that scared hare.

'You came early,' Roberts told Kate and me. 'Midnight is the official time for out gaudy little fiesta. That's when the fireworks begin.'

This was the part I couldn't get my head around: the switches from Mr East Coast Charm-School to Bite-Your-Ear Psychopath. From the needy, Woody Allen type guy who wants you to understand and empathise to the psycho with the knife and the box of matches.

Did I tell you about the matches?

They were right there on the dash beside the phone and the laptop computer, to the left of a miniature TV screen. I spotted them when Roberts roughly dragged

Angel out of the trunk and carried her to the front seat. He lifted her like she was a small kid, and she stayed scrunched up, her knees to her chest. Her rolled-up sweater showed the curve of her spine and twelve inches of pale, skinny flesh. When he sat her down, she crumpled forward, head in hands.

'I gotta give you credit,' Roberts said to Kate and me as he hustled us into the back seat behind Angel and took the driver's seat himself.

Not that we were going anywhere, so don't get the wrong impression. It's that he wanted us to relax and rest easy while he covered all the facts.

'You two are just kids.' He began with the compliments, pulling out a cigarette, reaching for the matches, then shaking his head and grinning. 'No naked flames until midnight,' he reminded himself. Back went the cigarette into the packet, nice and neat.

I saw Kate grasp the seat in front until her knuckles turned white.

'Just kids,' he resumed. 'How old? No, don't tell me. Fifteen? Sixteen? But you sure as hell beat the cops at their game. I wasn't too sure about the Hades link; maybe a shade too difficult. What d'you think?'

The bundle of shaking bones that had once been Angel Christian, Superstar, began to whimper and rock.

Kate took off her jacket, reached forward and put it around her shoulders.

'But you're bright,' Roberts went on. 'Bright enough to join Angel; minor stars in her galaxy, shining in the night sky.'

I grew sicker and sicker. It came over me in waves. My skin was covered in a cold sweat.

'Which means I can tell it like it is to you, because I know you'll understand. Once upon a time there was a TV show, and this TV show had an Angel in it and lots of little people who weren't angels.

'Now these little people were only in the show to get trampled on by Angel's pretty high-heeled shoes. And all went well for many years, and Angel grew rich, and the little, trampled people got kicked out on to the street after each show to try and pick up the tiny pieces of their shattered little lives.'

Angel moaned and shook. Kate leaned sideways against me and hid her face in my jacket. I put my arm around her. It was trembling more than it ever did when I fantasised this action.

OK, give us your once-upon-a-time fantasy stuff, I said to Roberts inside my head. I'm listening to footsteps coming down the alley, a fist hammering on a nearby door. Our psycho is so caught up in his fairy story, he doesn't catch the interruption.

'Then one day; surprise! A little person with a shattered life turns right around and works out a plan that he knows will make Angel learn the error of her ways. It involves a couple of other little people; namely the driver and, as it turns out, the help.'

Roberts paused to see what effect the story so far was having on Kate and me. He dipped into his pack of cigarettes and this time almost lit a match before he remembered.

I thought, *This is it. The whole thing's gonna go up*!

'Naughty!' He remembered just in time, then tapped the back of his own hand. 'You wanna know where the driver and the help figure?' he asked us.

'Pam is not the help, she's my sister!' Angel whimpered, still curled up in the front like a foetus.

'Hey, really!' Mock surprise from Campus-Man. Like he gives a damn.

'Jasper!' a voice in the alley called. 'Jasper Guziak! Hey man, open the door, I'm thirsty!'

'I know Stone from way back.' This time Roberts did frown at the disturbance. He wasn't going to let it ruin a good story, though. 'I arrange to meet him in a bar. In Hell's Kitchen, actually, after the gig.

'That was Tuesday the 14th. We talk a little and I

persuade Stone that little people don't always have to take it from the big people. He can be a big person too with several million of Angel's dollars behind him. A share in a kidnap deal is what I'm offering, if he plays his part, which is to go into the studio on the following night and say there's been an accident: Pam the Help has been rushed to the ER at Fortune City General.

'Angel is to grab her coat and go with him. But Stone isn't to drive to the hospital, he's to bring her in the Mercedes to Hell's Kitchen and to me, waiting out on the sidewalk with open arms.

'Perfect, except for one problem. On the drive across town, Angel starts to panic and Stone isn't quick enough to stop her taking out her phone and calling home. The maid, Rais, takes the call. Stone lets Angel get out a couple of sentences, including the word, "kidnap", before he grabs the phone. The idiot tells me this when he drops Angel off. So the deal's off, I tell him, unless he takes care of the maid. I don't care how.'

'Guziak, open the door! Gimme a drink!' The faint demand went on and on.

I felt Kate stiffen. She'd heard it too. We both recognised the slurred voice of Tommy Jett. Angel, though, was too far gone to hear anything.

'The thing is, Stone understands he doesn't get the

money unless he deals with the maid.' Roberts spelt it out for us. 'He also knows he's in it up to here.' He chopped his hand against his neck. 'Stone tells me I can trust him. And it turns out I can.' He grinned and shrugged.

'Unfortunately, on Thursday morning, the help – sorry, sister – who's more involved with Stone than I know, begins to jump to conclusions. Stone's been acting strange, I guess, since the night before, and by now Angel and the maid are both missing. Poor little help-sister thinks Stone's to blame. She doesn't know about me. First, she thinks he's killed them both. Then, what a relief; it turns out to be only the maid. She covers for Stone like a hero. It's true love. Stone covers for me. Now, that's true greed. He still thinks the money's gonna come through.'

'I'll pay!' Angel groaned, like she'd been through this a thousand times. 'Anything!'

Roberts reached out and stroked the back of her head. 'Poor Angel. This isn't about money. It's about much, much more!' He turned to us, frowning at the noise still going on in the alley; a drunk demanding a drink when the club was locked up and empty, staggering round the back of the lot to hammer on the service door. The drunk was spoiling Roberts' story. And nobody – not Rais or Pam, not Stone, and certainly not a drunken bum – was gonna spoil the climax.

'Wait here!' he told Angel and Kate, getting out of the car, coming round the back and dragging me out with him. 'In case you think of doing something stupid, like screaming for help,' he told Angel and Kate, 'I got a knife in my pocket and the kid is with me.'

The plan was to raise the garage door and tell the drunk to get lost. Maybe give him a kicking or worse, depending if it was Mr Bite-Your-Ear Psycho speaking.

Sometimes a crazy man's ego gets so big, it invades other parts of his brain. Like the bit that should have said, 'Go easy, it's only a bum making a noise in an alley.'

'Guziak, man, open the door!'

Roberts has turned into Action Man. He's striding down the alley to shut Tommy up.

I'm thinking, *Oh, great.* Tommy just has to take one look at me and recognise me for him to be in deep trouble too. I hang back behind Roberts as much as I can, with him keeping hold of my sleeve.

No way do I want a conversation with Tommy Jett unless I can get him to mind read all of a sudden. *'Tommy, get help. Angel's in the garage. Fetch the cops!'*

'Get out of here!' Roberts yells at Tommy, not

recognising Angel's ex, using his free hand to grab him by the shoulder.

Tommy staggers back from the narrow black door. He looks wrecked; with the dyed dark roots of his blond hair, the black stubble, the whisky eyes. 'Hey, man!' he says, pulling his scabby air-force pilot's jacket straight.

'The club's closed, OK!' Roberts turns him around in the alley, manhandles him past the fire escape. Tommy shoots out an arm and grabs the rail.

'I want to speak to Jasper,' he tells Roberts, straightening himself up again. 'Jasper and me go way back. We sometimes take a little drink after hours. So what's wrong with that?'

I notice him trying to focus on Roberts' face. 'Hey, didn't I see you on . . . ?'

'Beat it.' A big shove, a lot of bad language.

Tommy staggers a bit, and as he picks himself up, he sees me.

No! I yell, though I don't say a word. This is telepathy I'm talking here. *Don't even think about saying hi! Just call the cops!*

Either Tommy's not as smashed as he looks, or else whisky improves your ability to mind read. I see him do a double take. Then he gives me an invisible nod. *OK, Carter; got you!*

'Take it easy,' he tells Roberts. 'Man, I'm outta here.'

Sometimes you gotta believe the impossible. Namely, that Tommy saw enough of what was going on, to fetch help.

Mind you, he didn't see the Mercedes behind the closed door, or know about Kate and Angel still trapped in there. The Welcome to the Underworld message wouldn't mean a thing to him.

We went back in to see Kate take Roberts' box of matches from the dash and throw it on the floor. She stamped the matches into the oily puddles as he rolled the door down behind us and set the catch.

She really ground those little sticks of wood into the dirt. End of fiesta. No midnight fireworks. She looked scared but defiant in the yellow beam from the head-light.

Inside the car, Angel had sat up straight and pulled Kate's jacket tight around her shoulders. There was someone at home at last behind those big, dark eyes.

'Good thinking,' Brett said, coolly regarding the heap of soggy matches. Then he slipped his hand inside his jacket pocket and drew out a fifty cent, disposable, red see-through plastic lighter.

'All boy scouts carry a back-up,' he said.

* * *

Brett had the lighter resting in his left palm, his fingers wrapped around its narrow stem, his thumb flexed back, ready to strike the flint.

It looked like he was about to bring the celebrations forward by a few hours.

Make no mistake, he was ready to go up with it. The car, Angel, Kate and me, plus Roberts himself.

There were no footsteps, just a metallic scrape as the key went into the lock from the outside, a click as the mechanism worked.

Roberts reacted like someone shot him. As he wheeled round to check what was happening with the door lock, I grabbed his left arm with both hands and rammed it back against the wall. I was gonna beat that lighter out of his grasp if it was the last thing I did.

Angel screamed and screamed, while Kate ran to help her out of the front seat.

Drop it, I said! Drop it! The fingers stayed closed, the thumb tried to make contact with the flint.

The door slid up. Tommy Jett stood there with a fat, six feet tall, bald guy who turned out to be Jasper Guziak. Jasper was part-janitor, part hirer and firer of bar staff for Hell's Kitchen. He got there before the cops because he lived on the premises. The important part is, he owned a garage key.

Brett Roberts' left hand ended up a bloody pulp. His thumb never quite made it to the flint.

Tommy and Jasper came in like quarter-backs and floored him. But he got up again and my hands were still around his wrist, prising his fingers open.

Kate hustled Angel out into the alley. The two of them ran like hell from that gas-soaked garage on to Twenty Second Street, and I don't blame them for that.

Roberts put up a crazy man struggle. And that didn't surprise me either.

It took the bulk of Jasper Guziak and a smack on the chin from his Mike Tyson size fist to put him out.

The red plastic lighter falls from his hand on to the hood of the white car and then to the floor. It spins in the yellow headlight beam slower and slower until finally it stops . . .

LAST WORDS

For the first time ever, Angel's show on Tuesday 21st February went out live.

No pre-recording, no editing. The first and last time, Dad said, in more ways than one.

I asked him what he meant, but he wouldn't say.

Because it was a special occasion, he got out of hospital early in a wheelchair and was in the production gallery now. Carter and I made up part of the studio audience with Connie, Zoey and Zig. Special front-row seats, courtesy of Angelworks and an ecstatic Imelda Cabasin.

Zoey showed me a bracelet Zig had given her. It was a silver snake. The head and the tail met, there was a raised zig-zag pattern to make its scales. 'Nice,' I said. I was pleased for them as they sat holding hands.

Connie sat between me and Carter. Her deep red lipstick matched her nail polish, which co-ordinated with her purple blouse, which contrasted with her matching black jacket and trousers. Silver studs in her ears and nose. Some gothic girl.

'What's with this big announcement?' She leaned forward to speak along the row to Zoey. 'Did you read the newspaper? It said Angel plans to use the show to say something special!'

'Maybe it's about her and Tommy Jett.' Zoey guessed along the same lines as sixteen million other Americans tuned in to watch.

Sixteen million! That's what an abduction and four days in a car trunk does for viewing figures. One million extra for every twenty four hours.

And now the papers were talking reconciliation.

'Tommy Saves Angel!' was the headline. Or variations: 'Tommy is Angel's Guardian!' 'Angel's Ex in Surprise Rescue!'

Way down the page, Carter's name came into it, and I was described as 'Injured Angelworks producer Sean Brennan's fifteen year old daughter, Kate'. Can't they get anything right? I'm sixteen. And it's important.

As you can imagine, the photographers crowding round Heaven's Gate practically killed to get a good picture of Angel coming home. There were so many hundreds of flashlights going off at the same time they couldn't show the footage on the TV news; they said it might cause visual disturbance bad enough to set off epileptic attacks.

But Angel was home, and you could see from the newspapers that Tommy was in the car with her. Which is how come the reconciliation rumours got started.

Dad said it would take more than a Rambo-type rescue to put things right between Angel and Tommy. There was his drinking, for a start. And any 'B' list movie actor who might still be hanging around.

But Mom flew back this morning to JFK convinced that Angel and Tommy were back together. 'They plan to renew their vows in a beach ceremony in Phuket,' she was telling her clients. The news was already all over New York.

Tommy was in the studio now; up in the gallery with Dad. He'd taken a shave, managed a change of clothes.

Then Angel's theme music started to play.

The audience fell silent, the lights went up on a gold-edged screen that was raised to let the star step forward.

No guests on stage. No little people, as Brett Roberts would have said.

Was he watching this from his police cell? Were Harvey Stone and Pam Collins?

Angel was dressed in a dark green velvet trouser suit. It came up high under her neck and fastened Chinese style. She looked dainty and demure, and as she gazed into the camera, her brown eyes shone with what looked like tears.

The audience went crazy. She was back. She was unharmed. We all stood up and cheered her.

When we gave her the chance, she began to speak. There were the thanks: to God, to her team at Angelworks and especially to Sean. She thanked her fans for their goodwill messages and prayers, her mother, who was dead, but who had taught her how to survive a crisis. She thanked Tommy, but she didn't say anything about a marriage ceremony on a beach. And she thanked Carter and me.

The cameraman turned the camera on us.

Joey put his head to one side, glanced at me and grinned. He looked like he wished he was invisible. His mom, dad, sister and baby brother were at the back of the studio cheering and clapping.

I grinned back at him.

Oh, yeah, the special announcement.

Angel gave a long list of all the charities she wanted to donate money to and do events for: women's refuges, adoptive children's societies, counselling groups for kids from broken homes.

Then she broke sixteen million hearts.

She told us it was the last show she would ever do.

Four days in a car trunk in the company of Brett Roberts had convinced her that there were better things to do with the rest of her life than host a confessional chat show. Angelworks was going to branch out into more movie production work and into serious documentaries.

The audience was stunned.

I looked at Carter and I could tell we both approved the decision one hundred per cent. We might be alone among fifteen million, but then the rest hadn't stepped through that garage door into hell with us.

Angel had been there.

'Goodbye,' she said. 'That's it from the very last edition of "Angel" . . . Take care and look after your friends.'

Friends? Me and Carter . . . yeah, friends. Leave it at that.

TWO FOR JOY

Jenny Oldfield

Kate Brennan. Joey Carter.
Flirting with danger . . . and each other.

A teenager on the run, a hitman with a gun.
Ethan's dad is dead. And he's left a fortune
to his son. But if Ethan dies, the money
reverts to his stepmother. And she really
wants that inheritance. Can Kate and Carter
beat the wicked stepmother and save
Ethan's life?

THREE FOR A GIRL

Jenny Oldfield

Kate Brennan. Joey Carter.
Flirting with danger... and each other.

The golden girl of American tennis is under pressure. So when she fails to show up at the start of a major tournament, no one's too surprised. Just another crack-up. But has Lola *really* pushed the self-destruct button? Kate and Carter are convinced this is something more sinister. And, together, they're usually right . . .